The Empty House

Ruskin Bond has been writing for over sixty years, and now has over 120 titles in print—novels, collections of short stories, poetry, essays, anthologies and books for children. His first novel, *The Room on the Roof*, received the prestigious John Llewellyn Rhys Award in 1957. He has also received the Padma Shri (1999), the Padma Bhushan (2014) and two awards from Sahitya Akademi—one for his short stories and another for his writings for children. In 2012, the Delhi government gave him its Lifetime Achievement Award.

Born in 1934, Ruskin Bond grew up in Jamnagar, Shimla, New Delhi and Dehradun. Apart from three years in the UK, he has spent all his life in India, and now lives in Mussoorie with his adopted family.

The Empty House

Selected and Compiled by
RUSKIN BOND

RUPA

Published by
Rupa Publications India Pvt. Ltd 2016
7/16, Ansari Road, Daryaganj
New Delhi 110002

Sales centres:
Allahabad Bengaluru Chennai
Hyderabad Jaipur Kathmandu
Kolkata Mumbai

ISBN: 978-81-291-4239-9

First impression 2016

10 9 8 7 6 5 4 3 2 1

Contents

Introduction

Strange creatures that appear as if from nowhere, travelling companions with hair-raising supernatural tales, people with terrible deep dark secrets—these are some of the common threads in the stories in this collection. I must admit I am partial to stories where the suspense is heightened by the writer's use of exotic locations. Some poor man or woman dropped into this mysterious locale has to contend with terrible uncanny spectacles.

'The Empty House' is a classic story of this kind, though there the writer-narrator doesn't have to travel anywhere too far. His aunt summons him to come explore the empty house with her. It looks like every other house on that street but has a dreadful past and holds its secrets close. As soon as the narrators enter the house, they know that something or someone is watching them. A someone who clearly doesn't like their presence there.

The story of 'Chuniya, Ayah' is from Alice Perrin's highly readable and engaging collection of tales from her travels during the Raj. *East of Suez* is full of exciting and eccentric characters and the account of this ayah, in particular, shows that if she had stayed well away from children, it would have ended on a happier note for everyone.

Vengeful animals or those that carry the spirit of something out of the ordinary appear in a few stories. In 'The Return of Imray' there are plenty of such creatures, from deadly kraits to a dog who can sense the malevolent presence of a dead man. 'The White Wolf of the Hartz Mountains' is a particularly hair-raising story set in a stark landscape. The extreme anxiety of the children in the story, the desperation of the father dealing with poverty and his own instincts and then the appearance of the white wolf in their lonely and friendless lives have the makings of an exotic story of revenge and retribution.

I have included here some authors I have read extensively over the years—Kipling, Perrin, R.L. Stevenson. I do hope they are still read today, for their stories though old, contain ideas and thoughts that have lived on. They will appeal to anyone who likes a good tale. As for some of the others whose works are included here, maybe reading them in this book will make you go out and search out their other writings.

This collection is for every reader who has been mesmerized by the possibility of something extraordinary living and breathing out there that we barely sense as we go about our everyday lives. I hope you enjoy this collection as much as I had reading these stories once again while choosing them for you.

Ruskin Bond

The Return of Imray

Rudyard Kipling

> *The doors were wide, the story saith,*
> *Out of the night came the patient wraith,*
> *He might not speak, and he could not stir*
> *A hair of the Baron's minniver—*
> *Speechless and strengthless, a shadow thin,*
> *He roved the castle to seek his kin.*
> *And oh,'twas a piteous thing to see*
> *The dumb ghost follow his enemy!*
>
> THE BARON

Imray achieved the impossible. Without warning, for no conceivable motive, in his youth, at the threshold of his career he chose to disappear from the world—which is to say, the little Indian station where he lived.

Upon a day he was alive, well, happy, and in great evidence among the billiard-tables at his Club. Upon a morning, he was not, and no manner of search could make sure where he might be. He had stepped out of his place; he had not appeared at his office at the proper time, and his dog cart was not upon the public roads. For these reasons, and because he was hampering, in a microscopical degree, the administration of the Indian Empire, that Empire paused for one microscopical moment to make inquiry into the fate of Imray. Ponds were dragged, wells were plumbed, telegrams were despatched down the lines of railways and to the nearest seaport town—twelve hundred miles away; but Imray was not at the end of the drag-ropes nor the telegraph wires. He was gone, and his place knew him no more.

Then the work of the great Indian Empire swept forward, because it could not be delayed, and Imray from being a man became a mystery—such a thing as men talk over at their tables in the Club for a month, and then forget utterly. His guns, horses and carts were sold to the highest bidder. His superior officer wrote an altogether absurd letter to his mother, saying that Imray had unaccountably disappeared, and his bungalow stood empty.

After three or four months of the scorching hot weather had gone by, my friend Strickland, of the Police, saw fit to rent the bungalow from the native landlord. This was before he was engaged to Miss Youghal—an affair which has been described in another place—and while he was pursuing his investigations into native life. His own life was sufficiently peculiar, and men complained of his manners and customs. There was always food in his house, but there were no regular times for meals. He ate, standing up and walking about, whatever he might find at the sideboard, and this is not good for human beings. His domestic equipment was limited to six rifles, three shotguns, five saddles, and a collection of stiff-jointed mahseer-rods, bigger and stronger than the largest salmon-rods. These occupied half of his bungalow, and the other half was given up to Strickland and his dog Tietjens—an enormous Rampur slut who devoured daily the rations of two men. She spoke to Strickland in a language of her own; and whenever, walking abroad, she saw things calculated to destroy the peace of Her Majesty the Queen–Empress, she returned to her master and laid information. Strickland would take steps at once, and the end of his labours was trouble and fine and imprisonment for other people. The natives believed that Tietjens was a familiar spirit, and treated her with the great reverence that is born of hate and fear. One room in the bungalow was set apart for her special use. She owned a bedstead, a blanket, and a drinking-trough, and if any one came into Strickland's room at night her custom was to knock down the invader and give tongue till someone came with a light. Strickland owed his life to her, when he was on the frontier, in search of a local murderer, who came in the gray dawn to send Strickland much farther than the Andaman Islands. Tietjens caught the man as he was crawling into Strickland's tent with a dagger between his teeth; and after his record of iniquity was established in the eyes of the law he was hanged. From that date, Tietjens wore a collar of rough silver, and employed a monogram on her night-blanket; and the blanket was of double woven Kashmir cloth, for she was a delicate dog.

Under no circumstances would she be separated from Strickland; and once, when he was ill with fever, made great trouble for the doctors, because she did not know how to help her master and would not allow another creature to attempt aid. Macarnaght, of the Indian Medical Service, beat her over her head with a gun-butt before she could understand that she must give room for those who could give quinine.

A short time after Strickland had taken Imray's bungalow,

my business took me through that station, and naturally, the Club quarters being full, I quartered myself upon Strickland. It was a desirable bungalow, eight-roomed and heavily thatched against any chance of leakage from rain. Under the pitch of the roof ran a ceiling cloth which looked just as neat as a whitewashed ceiling. The landlord had repainted it when Strickland took the bungalow. Unless you knew how Indian bungalows were built, you would never have suspected that above the cloth lay the dark three-cornered cavern of the roof, where the beams and the underside of the thatch harboured all manner of rats, bats, ants, and foul things.

Tietjens met me in the verandah with a bay like the boom of the bell of St. Paul's, putting her paws on my shoulder to show she was glad to see me. Strickland had contrived to claw together a sort of meal which he called lunch, and immediately after it was finished went out about his business. I was left alone with Tietjens and my own affairs. The heat of the summer had broken up and turned to the warm damp of the rains. There was no motion in the heated air, but the rain fell like ramrods on earth, and flung up a blue mist when it splashed back. The bamboos, and the custard apples, the poinsettias, and the mango trees in the garden stood still while the warm water lashed through them, and the frogs began to sing among the aloe hedges. A little before the light failed, and when the rain was at its worst, I sat in the back verandah and heard the water roar from the eaves, and scratched myself because I was covered with the thing called prickly heat. Tietjens came out with me and put her head in my lap and was very sorrowful; so I gave her biscuits when tea was ready, and I took tea in the back verandah on account of the little coolness found there. The rooms of the house were dark behind me. I could smell

Strickland's saddlery and the oil on his guns, and I had no desire to sit among these things. My own servant came to me in the twilight, the muslin of his clothes clinging tightly to his drenched body, and told me that a gentleman had called and wished to see some one. Very much against my will, but only because of the darkness of the rooms, I went into the naked drawing room, telling my man to bring the lights. There might or might not have been a caller waiting—it seemed to me that I saw a figure by one of the windows—but when the lights came there was nothing save the spikes of the rain without, and the smell of the drinking earth in my nostrils. I explained to my servant that he was no wiser than he ought to be, and went back to the verandah to talk to Tietjens. She had gone out into the wet, and I could hardly coax her back to me; even with biscuits with sugar tops. Strickland came home, dripping wet, just before dinner, and the first thing he said was:

'Has anyone called?'

I explained, with apologies, that my servant had summoned me into the drawing room on a false alarm; or that some loafer had tried to call on Strickland, and thinking better of it had fled after giving his name. Strickland ordered dinner, without comment, and since it was a real dinner with a white tablecloth attached, we sat down.

At nine o'clock Strickland wanted to go to bed, and I was tired too. Tietjens, who had been lying underneath the table, rose up, and swung into the least exposed verandah as soon as her master moved to his own room, which was next to the stately chamber set apart for Tietjens. If a mere wife had wished to sleep out of doors in that pelting rain it would not have mattered; but Tietjens was a dog, and therefore the better animal. I looked at Strickland, expecting to see him flay her with a whip. He smiled queerly, as a man would smile after telling some unpleasant domestic tragedy. 'She has done this ever since I moved in here,' said he. 'Let her go.'

The dog was Strickland's dog, so I said nothing, but I felt all that Strickland felt in being thus made light of. Tietjens encamped outside my bedroom window, and storm after storm came up, thundered on the thatch, and died away. The lightning spattered the sky as a thrown egg spatters a barn door, but the light was pale blue, not yellow; and, looking through my split bamboo blinds, I could see the great dog standing, not sleeping, in the verandah, the hackles alift on her back and her feet anchored as tensely as the drawn wire-rope of a suspension bridge. In the very short pauses of the thunder I tried to sleep, but it seemed that someone wanted me very urgently. He, whoever he was, was trying to call me by name, but his voice was no more than a husky whisper. The thunder ceased, and Tietjens went into the garden and howled at the low moon. Somebody tried to open my door, walked about and about through the house and stood breathing heavily in the verandahs, and just when I was falling asleep I fancied that I heard a wild hammering and clamouring above my head or on the door.

I ran into Strickland's room and asked him whether he was ill, and had been calling for me. He was lying on his bed half dressed, a pipe in his mouth. 'I thought you'd come,' he said. 'Have I been walking round the house recently?'

I explained that he had been tramping in the dining room and the smoking room and two or three other places, and he laughed and told me to go back to bed. I went back to bed and slept till the morning, but through all my mixed dreams I was sure I was doing someone an injustice in not attending to his wants. What those wants were I could not tell; but a fluttering, whispering, bolt-fumbling, lurking, loitering. Someone was reproaching me for my slackness, and, half awake, I heard the howling of Tietjens in the garden and the threshing of the rain.

I lived in that house for two days. Strickland went to his office daily, leaving me alone for eight or ten hours with Tietjens for my only companion. As long as the full light lasted I was comfortable, and so was Tietjens; but in the twilight she and I moved into the back verandah and cuddled each other for company. We were alone in the house, but none the less it was much too fully occupied by a tenant with whom I did not wish to interfere. I never saw him, but I could see the curtains between the rooms quivering where he had just passed through; I could hear the chairs creaking as the bamboos sprung under a weight that had just quit them; and I could feel when I went to get a book from the dining room that somebody was waiting in the shadows of the front verandah till I should have gone away. Tietjens made the twilight more interesting by glaring into the darkened rooms with every hair erect, and following the motions of something that I could not see. She never entered the rooms, but her eyes moved interestedly and that was quite sufficient. Only when my servant came to trim the lamps and make all light and habitable, she would come in with me and spend her time sitting on her haunches, watching an invisible extra man as he moved about behind my shoulder. Dogs are cheerful companions.

I explained to Strickland, gently as might be, that I would go over to the Club and find for myself quarters there. I admired his hospitality, was pleased with his guns and rods, but I did not much care for his house and its atmosphere. He heard me out to the end, and then smiled very wearily, but without contempt, for he is a man who understands things. 'Stay on,' he said, 'and see what this thing means. All you have talked about I have known since I took the bungalow. Stay on and wait. Tietjens has left me. Are you going too?'

I had seen him through one little affair, connected with a heathen idol, that had brought me to the doors of a lunatic asylum, and I had no desire to help him through further experiences. He was a man to whom unpleasantnesses arrived as do dinners to ordinary people.

Therefore I explained more clearly than ever that I liked him immensely, and would be happy to see him in the daytime; but that I did not care to sleep under his roof. This was after dinner, when Tietjens had gone out to lie in the verandah.

"Pon my soul, I don't wonder,' said Strickland, with his eyes on the ceiling cloth. 'Look at that!'

The tails of two brown snakes were hanging between the cloth and the cornice of the wall. They threw long shadows in the lamplight.

'If you are afraid of snakes of course—' said Strickland.

I hate and fear snakes, because if you look into the eyes of any snake you will see that it knows all and more of the mystery of man's fall, and that it feels all the contempt that the Devil felt when Adam was evicted from Eden. Besides which, its bite is generally fatal, and it twists up trouser legs.

'You ought to get your thatch overhauled,' I said.

'Give me a mahseer-rod, and we'll poke them down.'

'They'll hide among the roofbeams,' said Strickland. 'I can't stand snakes overhead. I'm going up into the roof. If I shake them down, stand by with a cleaning rod and break their backs.'

I was not anxious to assist Strickland in his work, but I took the cleaning rod and waited in the dining room, while Strickland brought a gardener's ladder from the verandah, and set it against the side of the room.

The snake tails drew themselves up and disappeared. We could hear the dry rushing scuttle of long bodies running over the baggy ceiling cloth. Strickland took a lamp with him, while I tried to make clear to him the danger of hunting roof snakes between a ceiling cloth and a thatch, apart from the deterioration of property caused by ripping out ceiling cloths.

'Nonsense!' said Strickland. 'They're sure to hide near the walls by the cloth. The bricks are too cold for them, and the heat of the room is just what they like.' He put his hand to the corner of the stuff and ripped it from the cornice. It gave with a great sound of tearing, and Strickland put his head through the opening into the dark of the angle of the roof beams. I set my teeth and lifted the rod, for I had not the least knowledge of what might descend.

'H'm!' said Strickland, and his voice rolled and rumbled in the roof. 'There's room for another set of rooms up here, and, by Jove, someone is occupying 'em!'

'Snakes?' I said from below.

'No. It's a buffalo. Hand me up the two last joints of a mahseer-rod, and I'll prod it. It's lying on the main roof beam.'

I handed up the rod.

'What a nest for owls and serpents! No wonder the snakes live here,' said Strickland, climbing farther into the roof. I could see his elbow thrusting with the rod. 'Come out of that, whoever you are! Heads below there! It's falling.'

I saw the ceiling cloth nearly in the centre of the room bag with a shape that was pressing it downwards and downwards towards the lighted lamp on the table. I snatched the lamp out of danger and stood back. Then the cloth ripped out from the walls, tore, split, swayed, and shot down upon the table something that I dared not look at, till Strickland had slid down the ladder and was standing by my side.

He did not say much, being a man of few words; but he picked up the loose end of the tablecloth and threw it over the remnants on the table.

'It strikes me,' said he, putting down the lamp, 'our friend Imray has come back. Oh! you would, would you?'

There was a movement under the cloth, and a little snake wriggled out, to be back-broken by the butt of the mahseer-rod. I was sufficiently sick to make no remarks worth recording.

Strickland meditated, and helped himself to drinks. The arrangement under the cloth made no more signs of life.

'Is it Imray?' I said.

Strickland turned back the cloth for a moment, and looked.

'It is Imray,' he said; 'and his throat is cut from ear to ear.'

Then we spoke, both together and to ourselves: 'That's why he whispered about the house.'

Tietjens, in the garden, began to bay furiously. A little later her great nose heaved open the dining room door.

She sniffed and was still. The tattered ceiling cloth hung down almost to the level of the table, and there was hardly room to move away from the discovery.

Tietjens came in and sat down; her teeth bared under her lip and her forepaws planted. She looked at Strickland.

'It's a bad business, old lady,' said he. 'Men don't climb up into the roofs of their bungalows to die, and they don't fasten up the ceiling cloth behind 'em. Let's think it out.'

'Let's think it out somewhere else,' I said.

'Excellent idea! Turn the lamps out. We'll get into my room.'

I did not turn the lamps out. I went into Strickland's room first, and allowed him to make the darkness. Then he followed me, and we lit tobacco and thought. Strickland thought. I smoked furiously because I was afraid.

'Imray is back,' said Strickland. 'The question is—who killed Imray? Don't talk, I've a notion of my own. When I took this bungalow I took over most of Imray's servants. Imray was guileless and inoffensive, wasn't he?'

I agreed; though the heap under the cloth had looked neither one thing nor the other.

'If I call in all the servants they will stand fast in a crowd and lie like Aryans. What do you suggest?'

'Call 'em in one by one,' I said.

'They'll run away and give the news to all their fellows,' said Strickland. 'We must segregate 'em. Do you suppose your servant knows anything about it?'

'He may, for aught I know; but I don't think it's likely. He has only been here two or three days,' I answered. 'What's your notion?'

'I can't quite tell. How the dickens did the man get the wrong side of the ceiling cloth?'

There was a heavy coughing outside Strickland's bedroom door. This showed that Bahadur Khan, his body servant, had waked from sleep and wished to put Strickland to bed.

'Come in,' said Strickland. 'It's a very warm night, isn't it?'

Bahadur Khan, a great, green-turbaned, six foot Mahomedan, said that it was a very warm night; but that there was more rain pending, which, by his Honour's favour, would bring relief to the country.

'It will be so, if God pleases,' said Strickland, tugging off his boots. 'It is in my mind, Bahadur Khan, that I have worked thee remorselessly for many days—ever since that time when thou first earnest into my service. What time was that?'

'Has the Heaven-born forgotten? It was when Imray Sahib went secretly to Europe without warning given; and I—even I—came into the honoured service of the protector of the poor.'

'And Imray Sahib went to Europe?'

'It is so said among those who were his servants.'

'And thou wilt take service with him when he returns?'

'Assuredly, Sahib. He was a good master, and cherished his dependants.'

'That is true. I am very tired, but I go buck shooting tomorrow. Give me the little sharp rifle that I use for black buck; it is in the case yonder.'

The man stooped over the case; handed barrels, stock, and fore-end to Strickland, who fitted all together, yawning dolefully. Then he reached down to the gun case, took a solid-drawn cartridge, and slipped it into the breech of the '360 Express.

'And Imray Sahib has gone to Europe secretly! That is very strange, Bahadur Khan, is it not?'

'What do I know of the ways of the white man. Heaven-born?'

'Very little, truly. But thou shalt know more anon. It has reached me that Imray Sahib has returned from his so long journeyings, and that even now he lies in the next room, waiting his servant.'

'Sahib!'

The lamplight slid along the barrels of the rifle as they levelled themselves at Bahadur Khan's broad breast.

'Go and look!' said Strickland. 'Take a lamp. Thy master is tired, and he waits thee. Go!'

The man picked up a lamp, and went into the dining room, Strickland following, and almost pushing him with the muzzle of the rifle. He looked for a moment at the black depths behind the ceiling cloth; at the writhing snake under foot; and last, a gray glaze settling on his face, at the thing under the tablecloth.

'Hast thou seen?' said Strickland after a pause.

'I have seen. I am clay in the white man's hands. What does the Presence do?'

'Hang thee within the month. What else?'

'For killing him? Nay, Sahib, consider. Walking among us, his servants, he cast his eyes upon my child, who was four years old. Him he bewitched, and in ten days he died of the fever—my child!'

'What said Imray Sahib?'

'He said he was a handsome child, and patted him on the head; wherefore my child died. Wherefore I killed Imray Sahib in the twilight, when he had come back from office, and was sleeping. Wherefore I dragged him up into the roof beams and made all fast behind him. The Heaven-born knows all things. I am the servant of the Heaven-born.'

Strickland looked at me above the rifle, and said, in the vernacular, 'Thou art witness to this saying? He has killed.'

Bahadur Khan stood ashen gray in the light of the one lamp. The need for justification came upon him very swiftly. 'I am trapped,' he said, 'but the offence was that man's. He cast an evil eye upon my child, and I killed and hid him. Only such as are served by devils,' he glared at Tietjens, couched stolidly before him, 'only such could know what I did.'

'It was clever. But thou shouldst have lashed him to the beam with a rope. Now, thou thyself wilt hang by a rope. Orderly!'

A drowsy policeman answered Strickland's call. He was followed by another, and Tietjens sat wondrous still.

'Take him to the police station,' said Strickland. 'There is a case toward.'

'Do I hang, then?' said Bahadur Khan, making no attempt to escape, and keeping his eyes on the ground.

'If the sun shines or the water runs—yes!' said Strickland.

Bahadur Khan stepped back one long pace, quivered, and stood still. The two policemen waited further orders.

'Go!' said Strickland.

'Nay; but I go very swiftly,' said Bahadur Khan. 'Look! I am even now a dead man.'

He lifted his foot, and to the little toe there clung the head of the half-killed snake, firm fixed in the agony of death.

'I come of land-holding stock,' said Bahadur Khan, rocking where he stood. 'It were a disgrace to me to go to the public scaffold, therefore I take this way. Be it remembered that the Sahib's shirts are correctly enumerated, and that there is an extra piece of soap in his washbasin. My child was bewitched, and I slew the wizard. Why should you seek to slay me with the rope? My honour is saved, and—and—I die.'

At the end of an hour he died, as they die who are bitten by the little brown karait, and the policemen bore him and the thing under the tablecloth to their appointed places. All were needed to make clear the disappearance of Imray.

'This,' said Strickland, very calmly, as he climbed into bed, 'is called the nineteenth century. Did you hear what that man said?'

'I heard,' I answered. 'Imray made a mistake.'

'Simply and solely through not knowing the nature of the Oriental, and the coincidence of a little seasonal fever. Bahadur Khan had been with him for four years.'

I shuddered. My own servant had been with me for exactly that length of time. When I went over to my own room I found my man waiting, impassive as the copper head on a penny, to pull off my boots.

'What has befallen Bahadur Khan?' said I.

'He was bitten by a snake and died. The rest the Sahib knows,' was the answer.

'And how much of this matter hast thou known?'

'As much as might be gathered from One coming in in the twilight to seek satisfaction. Gently, Sahib. Let me pull off those boots.'

I had just settled to the sleep of exhaustion when I heard Strickland shouting from his side of the house—

'Tietjens has come back to her place!'

And so she had. The great deerhound was couched statelily on her own bedstead on her own blanket, while, in the next room, the idle, empty, ceiling cloth waggled as it trailed on the table.

Chunia, Ayah

Alice Perrin

'I hope you clearly understand that I do not believe in ghosts?'
The little grey-haired spinster paused and regarded me
with suspicion, and alarmed lest I should, after all, lose the story
I had been so carefully stalking, I vehemently reassured her on
the point, whereupon, to my relief, she continued—

'It certainly was a most extraordinary thing, and even now
I hardly know what to make of it, though it happened a long
time ago. One cold weather when I was in India keeping house
for my brother, I received a letter from a friend, begging me to
pay her a long promised visit. She wrote that her husband was
going into camp for a month to a part of his district where she
could not accompany him, so that she and her little girl would
be all alone, and I should be doing her a great kindness by
coming. So the end of it was I accepted the invitation, though I
greatly disliked leaving my brother to the tender mercies of the
servants, and after a long, hot journey arrived at my destination
at five o'clock one evening.

'My friend, Mrs Pollock, was on the platform to meet me,
and outside the station a bamboo cart was waiting, into which

we climbed, and were soon bowling along the hard, white road at a brisk pace. Mary at once began to relate anecdotes of her little girl, whose name was Dot—how tall she was for her age (twenty months!), how much she ate, what she tried to say, what the ayah said about her, and so on.

'Now I must confess that I am not very fond of children; I like them well enough in their proper place (if that is not too near me), but I do not know how to behave towards them, and am always nervous as to what they will do or say next. Therefore, fond as I was of Mary herself, the subject of her conversation did not particularly interest me. When we arrived at the house, she actually inquired which I would do first—see Dot or have some tea! I boldly elected for tea, as I was exceedingly tired and thirsty, and I also reflected that if I did not at once make a determined stand, I should be "Dot-ridden" for the remainder of my visit.

'After tea I was taken to my room, and Mary brought her treasure to me for exhibition. She was the most lovely child I had ever beheld, with a grave, sweet face that quite won my unmotherly heart, and for once my prejudices completely melted away. Mary put her into my arms and stood by in an ecstacy of pride and delight as I proceeded to tap the pin-cushion, rattle my keys and perform various idiotic antics in my efforts to amuse Dot, who, I felt sure, would set up a howl in a few moments. But she watched my foolish attempts to be entertaining with an attentive gravity that was quite embarrassing, and charmed though I was with the little creature, I felt relieved when she held out her arms to go back to her mother.

'Mary called for the ayah to come and take the child to her nursery, and a woman with a sullen, handsome face entered and took her charge away. I remarked that the ayah looked bad-tempered, upon which Mary assured me that she could trust the child anywhere with her, and that she was a perfect treasure.

'The next morning I was awakened by a soft little pat on my face, and, opening my eyes, I found Dot holding herself upright by the corner, of my pillow.

'"Why, little one, are you all alone?" I said, lifting her on to the bed, and then I discovered that her feet were wringing wet.

'She held up one wet little foot and examined it carefully, and then pointed to the bathroom door, which was open, and from where I lay I could see an overturned jug and streams of water on the floor—evidently Dot's handiwork. I put on my dressing gown and took the child to her mother, explaining what had happened, and Mary hastily pulled off the soaking little shoes and socks and called for the ayah, who presently entered, and stood silently watching her mistress.

'"What do you mean by leaving the child in this way?" exclaimed Mary, angrily, and gathering up Dot's shoes and socks, she threw them to the ayah, bidding her bring others that were dry. One of the little shoes struck the woman on the cheek, for Mary was annoyed and had flung them with unnecessary force, and never shall I forget the look on the ayah's face as she left the room to carry out the order. It was the face of a devil, but Mary did not see it, for she was busy rubbing the cold little feet in her hands.

'"Mary," I said impulsively, "I am sure the ayah is a brute. Do get rid of her. I never saw anything so dreadful as the look she gave you just now."

'"My dear," answered Mary, with good-humoured impatience, "you have taken an unreasonable dislike to Chunia. She knew she was in the wrong and felt ashamed of herself."

'So the matter dropped; but I could not get over my dislike

to Chunia, and as my visit wore on, and I became more and more attached to dear little Dot, I could hardly endure to see the child in her presence.

'My month with Mary passed quickly away, and I was really sorry when it was over, more especially as on my return home, my brother was called away unexpectedly on business, and I was left alone. I missed Dot more than I could have believed possible, for I had become ridiculously devoted to the small, round bundle of humanity, with the great dark eyes and short yellow curls, and my feelings are not to be described when the letter came from Mr Pollock giving me the awful news of the child's death.

'I read the letter over and over again, hardly able to believe it. The whole thing was so hideously sudden! I had only left Mary and Dot such a short time ago, and when last I had seen the child she was in her mother's arms on the platform of the railway station, kissing her little fat hands laboriously to me in farewell, and looking the picture of life and health.

'Poor Mr Pollock wrote in a heartbroken strain. It appeared that the child had strayed away one afternoon and must have fallen into the river, which ran past the bottom of the garden, for the little sun hat was found floating in the stream, and close to the water's edge lay a toy that she had been playing with all day. Every search had been made, but no further trace could be found. The poor mother was distracted with sorrow, and Mr Pollock had telegraphed for leave, as he meant to take her to England at once. He added that the ayah, Chunia, had been absent on three days leave when the dreadful accident happened, or, they both felt convinced, it would never have occurred at all. Mary, he wrote, sent me a message to beg me to take the woman into my service, as she could not endure the idea of one who had been so much with their darling going to strangers, for the poor woman had been a faithful servant, and was stricken and dumb with grief.

'I telegraphed at once that I would take Chunia willingly. I forgot my old antipathy to her, and only remembered that I should have someone about me who had known and loved the child so well. When the woman arrived I was quite shocked at her altered appearance. Her face seemed to have shrunk to half its former size, and her eyes looked enormous, and shone with a strange brilliancy. She was very quiet at first but burst into a flood of tears when I tried to speak to her of poor little Dot, so I gave it up, as I saw she could hardly bear the subject mentioned.

'She helped me to undress the first night, and then, instead of leaving the room, she stood looking at me without speaking.

'"What is it?" I inquired.

'"Memsahib," she said in a whisper, glancing over her shoulder, "may I sleep in your dressing room tonight?"

'I willingly gave her permission, for I saw that the woman's nerves were unstrung and that she needed companionship. Then I got into bed, and must have been asleep for some hours when I awoke thinking I had heard a shrill voice crying in the compound. I listened, and again it came, a high, beseeching wail. It was certainly the voice of a child, and the awful pleading and despair expressed in the sound was heart-rending. I felt sure some native baby had wandered into the grounds and was calling hopelessly for its mother.

'I lit a candle and went into my dressing room, where to my astonishment, I saw Chunia crouching against the outer door that led into the verandah, holding it fast with both hands as though she were shutting someone out.

'I asked what she was doing, and whether she knew whose child was crying outside. She sprang to her feet and answered sullenly that she had heard no child crying. I opened the door and went out into the verandah, but nothing was to be seen or heard, and I had no reply to my shouts of inquiry; so, concluding that it must have been my fancy, or perhaps some prowling animal, I returned to bed, and slept soundly for the rest of the night.

'The next evening I dined out, and on my return was surprised to hear someone talking in my dressing room. I hurried in, and again found Chunia kneeling in front of the outer door imploring somebody to "go away" at the top of her voice. Directly when she saw me she came towards me excitedly.

'"Oh! Memsahib!" she shrieked, "tell her to go away!"

'"Tell who?" I demanded.

'"Dottie-baba," she wailed, wringing her hands. "She cries to come to me—listen to her—listen!"

'She held her breath and waited, and I solemnly declare that as I stood and listened with her, I heard a child crying and moaning on the other side of the door. I was mute with horror and bewilderment, while the plaintive cry rose and fell, and then flinging the door open, I held the candle high above my head. There was no need of a light, for the moon was full, but no child could I see, and the verandah was quite empty. I determined to sift the matter to the bottom, so I went to the servants' quarters and called them all up. But no one could account for the crying of a child, and though the compound was thoroughly searched nothing was discovered. So the servants returned to their houses and I to my verandah, where I found Chunia in a most excited state.

'"Memsahib," she said, with her fists clenched and her eyes

starting out of her head, "will she go away if I tell you all about it?"

'"Yes, yes," I cried soothingly, "tell me what you like."

'She silently took my wrist and dragged me into the dressing room, shutting the door with the utmost caution.

'"Stand with your back against it," she whispered, "so that she cannot enter."

'I feared I was in the presence of a mad woman, so I did as she bade me, and waited quietly for her story. She walked up and down the room and began to speak in a kind of chant.

'"I did it," she sang. "I killed the child, little Dottie-baba, and she has followed me always. You heard her cry tonight and last night. The memsahib angered me the day she struck me with the shoe, and then a devil entered into my heart. I asked for leave, and went away, but it was too strong, it drew me back, and it said kill! Kill! I fought and struggled against the voice, but it was useless. So on the second day of my leave I crept back and hid among the bushes till I saw the child alone, and then I took her away and killed her. She was so glad to see me, and laughed and talked, but when she saw the devil in my eyes she grew frightened, and cried just as you heard her cry tonight. I took her little white neck in my hands—see memsahib, how large and strong my hands are—and I pressed and pressed until the child was dead, and then the devil left me. I looked and saw what I had done. I could not unclasp her fingers from my skirt, they clung so tightly, so I took it off and wrapped her in it—"

'The woman stopped suddenly. I had listened in silence, repressing the exclamations of horror that rose to my lips.

'"What did you do then?" I asked. Chunia looked wildly round.

'"I forget," she murmured; "the river, I ran quickly to the river—"

'Then there came a shriek from the dry, parched lips, and then flinging her arms above her head she fell at my feet unconscious and foaming at the mouth.

'Afterwards Chunia was found to be raving mad, and the doctor expressed his opinion that she must have been in a more or less dangerous state for some months past. I told him of her terrible confession to me, but he said that possibly the whole thing was a delusion on her part.

'I went to see her once after she had been placed under restraint, but the sight was so saddening that I never went again. She was seated on the floor of her prison patting an imaginary baby to sleep, croning the quaint little lullaby that ayahs always use, and when I spoke to her she only gazed at me with dull, vacant eyes, and continued the monotonous chant as though she had not seen me at all.

'And the child you heard crying?' I ventured to ask.

'"Oh! How can I tell what it was? I don't know," she answered with impatient perplexity. "I can't believe that it was the spirit of little Dot, and yet—and yet—what was it?"

From *East of Suez* (1926)

The Empty House

Algernon Blackwood

Certain houses, like certain persons, manage somehow to proclaim at once their character for evil. In the case of the latter, no particular feature need betray them; they may boast an open countenance and an ingenuous smile; and yet a little of their company leaves the unalterable conviction that there is something radically amiss with their being: that they are evil. Willy nilly) they seem to communicate an atmosphere of secret and wicked thoughts which makes those in their immediate neighbourhood shrink from them as from a thing diseased.

And, perhaps, with houses the same principle is operative, and it is the aroma of evil deeds committed under a particular roof, long after the actual doers have passed away, that makes the gooseflesh come and the hair rise. Something of the original passion of the evil-doer, and of the horror felt by his victim, enters the heart of the innocent watcher, and he becomes suddenly conscious of tingling nerves, creeping skin, and a chilling of the blood. He is terror-stricken without apparent cause.

There was manifestly nothing in the external appearance of this particular house to bear out the tales of the horror that was said to reign within. It was neither lonely nor unkempt. It stood, crowded into a corner of the square, and looked exactly like the houses on either side of it. It had the same number of windows as its neighbours; the same balcony overlooking the gardens; the same white steps leading up to the heavy black front door; and, in the rear, there was the same narrow strip of green, with neat box borders, running up to the wall that divided it from the backs of the adjoining houses. Apparently, too, the number of chimney pots on the roof was the same; the breadth and angle of the eaves; and even the height of the dirty area railings.

And yet this house in the square, that seemed precisely similar to its fifty ugly neighbours, was as a matter of fact entirely different—horribly different.

Wherein lay this marked, invisible difference is impossible to say. It cannot be ascribed wholly to the imagination, because persons who had spent some time in the house, knowing nothing of the facts, had declared positively that certain rooms were so disagreeable they would rather die than enter them again, and that the atmosphere of the whole house produced in them symptoms of a genuine terror; while the series of innocent tenants who had tried to live in it and been forced to decamp at the shortest possible notice, was indeed little less than a scandal in the town.

When Shorthouse arrived to pay a 'weekend' visit to his Aunt Julia in her little house on the seafront at the other end of the town, he found her charged to the brim with mystery and excitement. He had only received her telegram that morning, and he had come anticipating boredom; but the moment he touched her hand and kissed her apple-skin wrinkled cheek, he caught the first waves of her electrical condition. The impression deepened when he learned that there were to be no other visitors, and that he had been telegraphed for with a very special object.

Something was in the wind, and the 'something' would doubtless bear fruit; for this elderly spinster aunt, with a mania for psychical research, had brains as well as will power, and by hook or by crook she usually managed to accomplish her ends. The revelation was made soon after tea, when she sidled close up to him as they paced slowly along the seafront in the dusk.

'I've got the keys,' she announced in a delighted, yet half awesome voice. 'Got them till Monday!'

'The keys of the bathing-machine, or—?' he asked innocently; looking from the sea to the town. Nothing brought her so quickly to the point as feigning stupidity.

'Neither,' she whispered. 'I've got the keys of the haunted house in the square—and I'm going there tonight.'

Shorthouse was conscious of the slightest possible tremor down his back. He dropped his teasing tone. Something in her voice and manner thrilled him. She was in earnest.

'But you can't go alone—' he began.

'That's why I wired for you,' she said with decision.

He turned to look at her. The ugly, lined, enigmatical face was alive with excitement. There was the glow of genuine enthusiasm round it like a halo. The eyes shone. He caught another wave of her excitement, and a second tremor, more marked than the first, accompanied it.

'Thanks, Aunt Julia,' he said politely; 'thanks awfully.'

'I should not dare to go quite alone,' she went on, raising her voice; 'But with you I should enjoy it immensely You're afraid of nothing, I know.'

'Thanks so much,' he said again. 'Er—is anything likely to happen?'

'A great deal *has* happened,' she whispered, 'though it's been most cleverly hushed up. Three tenants have come and ,one in the last few months, and the house is said to be empty for good now.'

In spite of himself, Shorthouse became interested. His aunt was so very much in earnest.

'The house is very old indeed,' she went on, 'and the story—an unpleasant one—dates a long way back. It has to do with a murder committed by a jealous stableman who had some affair with a servant in the house. One night he managed to secrete himself in the cellar, and when everyone was asleep, he crept upstairs to the servants' quarters, chased the girl down to the next landing, and before anyone could come to the rescue threw her bodily over the bannisters into the hall below.'

'And the stableman—?'

'Was caught, I believe, and hanged for murder; but it all happened a century ago, and I've not been able to get more details of the story.'

Shorthouse now felt his interest thoroughly aroused but, though he was not particularly nervous for himself, he hesitated a little on his aunt's account.

'On one condition,' he said at length.

'Nothing will prevent my going,' she said firmly; 'but I may as well hear your condition.'

'That you guarantee your power of self-control if anything really horrible happens. I mean—that you are sure you won't get too frightened.'

'Jim,' she said scornfully, 'I'm not young, I know, nor are my nerves; but *with you* I should be afraid of nothing in the world!'

This, of course, settled it, for Shorthouse had no pretensions to being other than a very ordinary young man, and an appeal to his vanity was irresistible. He agreed to go.

Instinctively; by a sort of subconscious preparation, he kept himself and his forces well in hand the whole evening, compelling an accumulative reserve of control by that nameless inward process of gradually putting all the emotions away and turning the key upon them—a process difficult to describe, but wonderfully effective, as all men who have lived through severe trials of the inner man well understand. Later, it stood him in good stead.

But it was not until half past ten, when they stood in the hall, well in the glare of friendly lamps and still surrounded by comforting human influences, that he had to make the first call upon this store of collected strength. For, once the door was closed, and he saw the deserted silent street stretching away white in the moonlight before them, it came to him clearly that the real test that night would be in dealing with *two fears* instead of one. He would have to carry his aunt's fear as well as his own. And, as he glanced down at her sphinx-like countenance and realized that it might assume no pleasant aspect in a rush of real terror, he felt satisfied with only one thing in the whole adventure—that he had confidence in his own will and power to stand against any shock that might come.

Slowly they walked along the empty streets of the town; a bright autumn moon silvered the roofs, casting deep shadows; there was no breath of wind; and the trees in the formal gardens by the seafront watched them silently as they passed along. To his aunt's occasional remarks Shorthouse made no reply; realizing that she was simply surrounding herself with mental buffers—saying ordinary things to prevent herself thinking of extraordinary things. Few windows showed lights, and from scarcely a single chimney came smoke or sparks. Shorthouse had already begun to notice everything, even the smallest details. Presently they stopped at the street corner and looked up at the name on the side of the house full in the moonlight, and with one accord, but without remark, turned into the square and crossed over to the side of it that lay in shadow.

'The number of the house is thirteen,' whispered a voice at his side; and neither of them made the obvious reference, but passed across the broad sheet of moonlight and began to march up the pavement in silence.

It was about half-way up the square that Shorthouse felt an arm slipped quietly but significantly into his own, and knew then that their adventure had begun in earnest, and that his companion was already yielding imperceptibly to the influences against them. She needed support.

A few minutes later they stopped before a tall, narrow house that rose before them into the night, ugly in shape and painted a dingy white. Shutterless windows, without blinds, stared down upon them, shining here and there in the moonlight. There were weather streaks in the wall and cracks in the paint, and the balcony bulged out from the first floor a little unnaturally. But, beyond this generally forlorn appearance of an unoccupied house, there was nothing at first sight to single out this particular mansion for the evil character it had most certainly acquired.

Taking a look over their shoulders to make sure they had not been followed, they went boldly up the steps and stood against the huge black door that fronted them forbiddingly. But the first wave of nervousness was now upon them, and Shorthouse fumbled a long time with the key before he could fit it into the lock at all. For a moment, if truth were told, they both hoped it would not open, for they were a prey to various unpleasant emotions as they stood there on the threshold of their ghostly adventure. Shorthouse, shuffling with the key and hampered by the steady weight on his arm, certainly felt the solemnity of the moment. It was as if the whole world—for all experience seemed at that instant concentrated in his own consciousness—were listening to the grating noise of that key. A stray puff of wind wandering down the empty street woke a momentary rustling in the trees behind them, but otherwise this rattling of the key was the only sound audible; and at last it turned in the lock and the heavy door swung open and revealed a yawning gulf of darkness beyond.

With a last glance at the moonlit square, they passed quickly in, and the door slammed behind them with a roar that echoed prodigiously through empty halls and passages. But, instantly, with the echoes, another sound made itself heard, and Aunt Julia leaned suddenly so heavily upon him that he had to take a step backwards to save himself from falling.

A man had coughed close beside them—so close that it seethed they must have been actually by his side in the darkness.

With the possibility of practical jokes in his mind, Shorthouse at once swung his heavy stick in the direction of the sound; but it met nothing more solid than air. He heard his aunt give a little gasp beside him.

'There's someone here,' she whispered: 'I heard him.'

'Be quiet!' he said sternly. 'It was nothing but the noise of the front door.'

'Oh! Get a light—quick!' she added, as her nephew fumbling with a box of matches, opened it upside down and let them all fall with a rattle on to the stone floor.

The sound, however, was not repeated; and there was no evidence of retreating footsteps. In another minute they had a candle burning, using an empty end of a cigar case as a holder; and when the first flare had died down he held the impromptu lamp aloft and surveyed the scene. And it was dreary enough in all conscience, for there is nothing more desolate in all the abodes of men than an unfurnished house dimly lit, silent, and forsaken, and yet tenanted by rumour with the memories of evil and violent histories.

They were standing in a wide hallway; on their left was the open door of a spacious dining room, and in front the hall ran, ever narrowing, into a long, dark passage that led apparently to the top of the kitchen stairs. The broad uncarpeted staircase rose in a sweep before them, everywhere draped in shadows, except for a single spot about half-way up where the moonlight came in through the window and fell on a bright patch on the boards. This shaft of light shed a faint radiance above and below it, lending to the objects within its reach a misty outline that was infinitely more suggestive and ghostly than complete darkness. Filtered moonlight always seems to paint faces on the surrounding gloom, and as Shorthouse peered up into the well of darkness and thought of the countless empty rooms and passages in the upper part of the old house, he caught himself longing again for the safety of the moonlit square, or the cosy, bright drawing room they had left an hour before. Then realizing that these thoughts were dangerous, he thrust them away again and summoned all his energy for concentration on the present.

'Aunt Julia,' he said aloud, severer; 'we must now go through the house from top to bottom and make a thorough search.'

The echoes of his voice died away slowly all over the building, and in the intense silence that followed he turned to

look at her. In the candlelight he saw that her face was already
ghastly pale; but she dropped his arm for a moment and said
in a whisper, stepping close in front of him—

'I agree. We must be sure there's no one hiding. That's
the first thing.'

She spoke with evident effort, and he looked at her with
admiration.

'You feel quite sure of yourself? It's not too late—'

'I think so,' she whispered, her eyes shifting nervously
toward the shadows behind. 'Quite sure, only one thing—'

'What's that?'

'You must never leave me alone for an instant.'

'As long as you understand that any sound or appearance
must be investigated at once, for to hesitate means to admit
fear. That is fatal.'

'Agreed,' she said, a little shakily; after a moment's
hesitation. 'I'll try—'

Arm in arm, Shorthouse holding the dripping candle and
the stick, while his aunt carried the cloak over her shoulders,
figures of utter comedy to all but themselves, they began a
systematic search. Stealthily, walking on tiptoe and shading the
candle lest it should betray their presence through the shutterless
windows, they went first into the big dining room. There was
not a stick of furniture to be seen. Bare walls, ugly mantelpieces
and empty grates stared at them. Everything, they felt, resented
their intrusion, watching them, as it were, with veiled eyes;
whispers followed them; shadows flitted noiselessly to right and
left; something seemed ever at their back, watching, waiting an
opportunity to do them injury. There was the inevitable sense
that operations which went on when the room was empty had
been temporarily suspended till they were well out of the way

again. The whole dark interior of the old building seemed to become a malignant Presence that rose tip, warning them to desist and mind their own business; every moment the strain on the nerves increased.

Out of the gloomy dining room they passed through large folding doors into a sort of library or smoking room, wrapt equally in silence, darkness, and dust; and from this they regained the hall near the top of the back stairs.

Here a pitch black tunnel opened before them into the lower regions, and—it must be confessed—they hesitated. But only for a minute. With the worst of the night still to come it was essential to turn from nothing. Aunt Julia stumbled at the top step of the dark descent, ill-lit by the flickering candle, and even Shorthouse felt at least half the decision go out of his legs.

'Come on!' he said peremptorily, and his voice ran on and lost itself in the dark, empty spaces below.

'I'm coming,' she faltered, catching his arm with unnecessary violence.

They went a little unsteadily down the stone steps, a cold, damp air meeting them in the face, close and malodorous. The kitchen, into which the stairs led along a narrow passage, was large, with a lofty ceiling. Several doors opened out of it—some into cupboards with empty jars still standing on the shelves, and others into horrible little ghostly back offices, each colder and less inviting than the last. Black beetles scurried over the floor, and once, when they knocked against a deal table standing in a corner, something about the size of a cat jumped down with a rush and fled, scampering across the stone floor into the darkness. Everywhere there was a sense of recent occupation, an impression of sadness and gloom.

Leaving the plain kitchen, they next went towards the

scullery. The door was standing ajar, and as they pushed it open to its full extent Aunt Julia uttered a piercing scream, which she instantly tried to stifle by placing her hand over her mouth. For a second Shorthouse stood stock-still, catching his breath. He felt as if his spine had suddenly become hollow and someone had filled it with particles of ice.

Facing them, directly in their way between the doorposts, stood the figure of a woman. She had dishevelled hair and wildly staring eyes, and her face was terrified and white as death.

She stood there motionless for the space of a single second. Then the candle flickered and she was gone—gone utterly—and the door framed nothing but empty darkness.

'Only the beastly jumping candlelight,' he said quickly, in a voice that sounded like someone else's and was only half under control. 'Come on, aunt. There's nothing there.'

He dragged her forward. With a clattering of feet and a great appearance of boldness they went on, but over his body the skin moved as if crawling ants covered it, and he knew by the weight on his arm that he was supplying the force of locomotion for two. The scullery was cold, bare, and empty; more like a large prison cell than anything else. They went round it, tried the door into the yard, and the windows, but found them all fastened securely. His aunt moved beside him like a person in a dream. Her eyes were tightly shut, and she seemed merely to follow the pressure of his arm. Her courage filled him with amazement. At the same time he noticed that a certain odd change had come over her face, a change which somehow evaded his power of analysis.

'There's nothing here, aunty,' he repeated aloud quickly 'Let's go upstairs and see the rest of the house. Then we'll choose a room to wait up in.'

She followed him obediently keeping close to his side, and they locked the kitchen door behind them. It was a relief to get up again. In the hall there was more light than before, for the moon had travelled a little further down the stairs. Cautiously they began to go up into the dark vault of the upper house, the boards creaking under their weight.

On the first floor they found the large double drawing rooms, a search of which revealed nothing. Here also was no sign of furniture or recent occupancy; nothing but dust and neglect and shadows. They opened the big folding doors between front and back drawing rooms and then came out again to the landing and went on upstairs.

They had not gone up more than a dozen steps when they both simultaneously stopped to listen, looking into each other's eyes with a new apprehension across the flickering candle flame. From the room they had left hardly ten seconds before came the sound of doors quietly closing. It was beyond all question; they heard the booming noise that accompanies the shutting of heavy doors, followed by the sharp catching of the latch.

'We must go back and see,' said Shorthouse briefly, in a low tone, and turning to go downstairs again.

Somehow she managed to drag after him, her feet catching in her dress, her face livid.

When they entered the front drawing rooms it was plain that the folding doors had been closed—half a minute before. Without hesitation Shorthouse opened them. He almost expected to see someone facing him in the back room; but only darkness and cold air met him. They went through both rooms, finding nothing unusual. They tried in every way to make the doors close of themselves, but there was not wind enough even to set the candle flame flickering. The doors would not move without strong pressure. All was silent as the grave. Undeniably the rooms were utterly empty; and the house utterly still.

'It's beginning.' Whispered a voice at his elbow which he hardly recognized as his aunt's.

He nodded acquiescence, taking out his watch to note the time. It was fifteen minutes before midnight; he made the entry of exactly what had occurred in his notebook, setting the candle in its case upon the floor in order to do so. It took a moment or two to balance it safely against the wall.

Aunt Julia always declared that at this moment she was not actually watching him, but had turned her head towards the inner room, where she fancied she heard something moving; but, at any rate, both positively agreed that there came a sound of rushing feet, heavy and very swift—and the next instant the candle was out!

But to Shorthouse himself had come more than this, and he has always thanked his fortunate stars that it came to him alone and not to his aunt too. For, as he rose from the stooping position of balancing the candle, and before it was actually extinguished, a face thrust itself forward so close to his own that he could almost have touched it with his lips. It was a face working with passion; a man's face, dark, with thick features, and angry, savage eyes. It belonged to a common man, and it was evil in its ordinary normal expression, no doubt, but as he saw it, alive with intense, aggressive emotion it was a malignant and terrible human countenance.

There was no movement of the air; nothing but the sound of rushing feet—stockinged or muffled feet; the apparition of the face; and the almost simultaneous extinguishing of the candle.

In spite of himself, Shorthouse uttered a little cry, nearly losing his balance as his aunt clung to him with her whole weight in one moment of real, uncontrollable terror. She made no sound, but simply seized him bodily. Fortunately, however, she had seen nothing, but had only heard the rushing feet, for her control returned almost at once, and he was able to disentangle himself and strike a match.

The shadows ran away on all sides before the glare, and his aunt stooped down and groped for the cigar case with the precious candle. Then they discovered that the candle had not been *blown* out at all; it had been *crushed* out. The wick was pressed down into the wax, which was flattened as if by some smooth, heavy instrument.

How his companion so quickly overcame her terror, Shorthouse never properly understood; but his admiration for her self-control increased tenfold, and at the same time served to feed his own dying flame—for which he was undeniably grateful. Equally inexplicable to him was the evidence of physical force they had just witnessed. He at once suppressed the memory of stories he had heard of 'physical mediums' and their dangerous phenomena; for if these were true, and either his aunt or himself was unwittingly a physical medium, it meant that they were simply aiding to focus the forces of a haunted house already charged to the brim. It was like walking with unprotected lamps among uncovered stores of gunpowder.

So, with as little reflection as possible, he simply relit the candle and went up to the next floor. The arm in his trembled, it is true, and his own tread was often uncertain, but they went on with thoroughness, and after a search revealing nothing they climbed the last flight of stairs to the top floor of all.

Here they found a perfect nest of small servants' rooms, with broken pieces of furniture, dirty cane-bottomed chairs, chests of drawers, cracked mirrors, and decrepit bedsteads. The rooms had low sloping ceilings already hung here and there with cobwebs, small windows, and badly plastered walls—a depressing and dismal region which they were glad to leave behind.

It was on the stroke of midnight when they entered a small room on the third floor, close to the top of the stairs, and arranged to make themselves comfortable for the remainder of their adventure. It was absolutely bare, and was said to be the room—then used as a clothes closet—into which the infuriated groom had chased his victim and finally caught her. Outside, across the narrow landing, began the stairs leading up to the floor above, and the servants' quarters where they had just searched.

In spite of the chilliness of the night there was something in the air of this room that cried for an open window. But there was more than this. Shorthouse could only describe it by saving that he felt less master of himself here than in any other part of the house. There was something that acted directly on the nerves, tiring the resolution, enfeebling the will. He was conscious of this result before he had been in the room five minutes, and it was in the short time they stayed there that he suffered the wholesale depletion of his vital forces, which was, for himself, the chief horror of the whole experience.

They put the candle on the floor of the cupboard, leaving the door a few inches ajar, so that there was no glare to confuse the eyes, and no shadow to shift about on walls and ceiling. Then they spread the cloak on the floor and sat down to wait, with their backs against the wall.

Shorthouse was within two feet of the door on to the landing; his position commanded a good view of the main staircase leading down into the darkness, and also of the beginning of the servants' stairs going to the floor above; the heavy stick lay beside him within easy reach.

The moon was now high above the house. Through the open window they could see the comforting stars like friendly eyes watching in the sky. One by one the clocks of the town struck midnight, and when the sounds died away the deep silence of a windless night fell again over everything. Only the boom of the sea, far away and lugubrious, filled the air with hollow murmurs.

Inside the house the silence became awful; awful, he thought, because any minute now it might be broken by sounds portending terror. The strain of waiting told more and more severely on the nerves; they talked in whispers when they talked at all, for their voices aloud sounded queer and unnatural. A chilliness, not altogether due to the night air, invaded the room, and made them cold. The influences against them, whatever these might be, were slowly robbing them of self-confidence, and the power of decisive action: their forces were on the wane, and the possibility of real fear took on a new and terrible meaning. He began to tremble for the elderly woman by his side, whose pluck could hardly save her beyond a certain extent.

He heard the blood singing in his veins. It sometimes seemed so loud that he fancied it prevented his hearing properly certain other sounds that were beginning very faintly to make themselves audible in the depths of the house. Every time he fastened his attention on these sounds, they instantly ceased. They certainly came no nearer. Yet he could not rid himself of the idea that movement was going on somewhere in the lower regions of the house. The drawing room floor, where the door had been so strangely closed, seemed too near; the sounds were further off than that. He thought of the great kitchen, with the scurrying black beetles, and of the dismal little scullery;

but, somehow or other, they did not seem to come from there either. Surely they were not *outside* the house!

Then, suddenly, the truth flashed into his mind, and for the space of a minute he felt as if his blood had stopped flowing and turned to ice.

The sounds were not downstairs at all; they were *upstairs*— upstairs, somewhere among those horrid gloomy little servants' rooms with their bits of broken furniture, low ceilings, and cramped windows—upstairs where the victim had first been disturbed and stalked to her death.

And the moment he discovered where the sounds were, he began to hear them more clearly. It was the sound of feet, moving stealthily along the passage overhead, in and out among the rooms, and past the furniture.

He turned quickly to steal a glance at the motionless figure seated beside him, to note whether she had shared his discovery The faint candlelight coming through the crack in the cupboard door, threw her strongly-marked face into vivid relief against the white of the wall. But it was something else that made him catch his breath and stare again. An extraordinary something had come into her face and seemed to spread over her features like a mask; it smoothed out the deep lines and drew the skin everywhere a little tighter so that the wrinkles disappeared; it brought into the face—with the sole exception of the old eyes—an appearance of youth and almost of childhood.

He stared in speechless amazement—amazement that was dangerously near to horror. It was his aunt's face indeed, but it was her face of forty years ago, the vacant, innocent face of a girl. He had heard stories of that strange effect of terror which could wipe a human countenance clean of other emotions, obliterating all previous expression; but he had never realized that it could be literally true, or could mean anything so simply horrible as what he now saw for the dreadful signature of overmastering fear was written plainly in that utter vacancy of the girlish face beside him; and when, feeling his intense gaze, she turned to look at him, he instinctively closed his eyes tightly to shut out the sight.

Yet, when he turned a minute later, his feelings well in hand, he saw to his intense relief another expression; his aunt was smiling, and though the face was deathly white, the awful veil had lifted and the normal look was returning.

'Anything wrong?' was all he could think of to say at the moment. And the answer was eloquent, coming from such a woman.

'I feel cold—and a little frightened,' she whispered.

He offered to close the window, but she seized hold of him and begged him not to leave her side even for an instant.

'It's upstairs, I know,' she whispered, with an odd half laugh; 'but I can't possibly go up.'

But Shorthouse thought otherwise, knowing that in action lay their best hope of self-control.

He took the brandy flask and poured out a glass of neat spirit, stiff enough to help anybody over anything. She swallowed it with a little shiver. His only idea now was to get out of the house before her collapse became inevitable; but this could not safely be done by turning tail and running from the enemy. Inaction was no longer possible; every minute he was growing less master of himself, and desperate, aggressive measures were imperative without further delay. Moreover, the action must be taken *towards* the enemy; not away from it; the climax, if necessary and unavoidable, would have to be faced boldly. He could do it now; but in ten minutes he might not have the force left to act for himself, much less for both!

Upstairs, the sounds were meanwhile becoming louder and closer, accompanied by occasional creaking of the boards. Someone was moving stealthily about, stumbling now and then awkwardly against the furniture.

Waiting a few moments to allow the tremendous dose of spirits to produce its effect, and knowing this would last but a short time under the circumstances, Shorthouse then quietly got on his feet, saying in a determined voice—

'Now, Aunt Julia, we'll go upstairs and find out what all this noise is about. You must come too. It's what we agreed.'

He picked tip his stick and went to the cupboard for the candle. A limp form rose shakily beside him breathing hard, and he heard a voice say very faintly something about being 'ready to come'. The woman's courage amazed him; it was so much greater than his own: and, as they advanced, holding aloft the dripping candle, some subtle force exhaled from this trembling, white-faced old woman at his side that was the true source of his inspiration. It held something really great that shamed him and gave him the support without which he would have proved far less equal to the occasion.

They crossed the dark landing, avoiding with their eyes the deep black space over the banisters. Then they began to mount the narrow staircase to meet the sounds which, minute by minute, grew louder and nearer. About half-way up the stairs Aunt Julia stumbled and Shorthouse turned to catch her by the arm, and just at that moment there came a terrific crash in the servants' corridor overhead. It was instantly followed by a shrill, agonized scream that was a cry of terror and a cry for help melted into one.

Before they could move aside, or go down a single step,

someone came rushing along the passage overhead, blundering horribly, racing madly, at full speed, three steps at a time, down the very staircase where they stood. The steps were light and uncertain; but close behind them sounded the heavier tread of another person, and the staircase seemed to shake.

Shorthouse and his companion just had time to flatten themselves against the wall when the jumble of flying steps was upon them, and two persons, with the slightest possible interval between them, dashed past at full speed. It was a perfect whirlwind of sound breaking in upon the midnight silence of the empty building.

The two runners, pursuer and pursued, had passed clean through them where they stood, and already with a thud the boards below had received first one, then the other. Yet they had seen absolutely nothing—not a hand, or arm, or face, or even a shred of flying clothing.

There came a second's pause. Then the first one, the lighter of the two, obviously the pursued one, ran with uncertain footsteps into the little room which Shorthouse and his aunt had just left. The heavier one followed. There was a sound of scuffling, gasping, and smothered screaming; and then out on to the landing came the step—of a single person treading weightily.

A dead silence followed for the space of half a minute, and then was heard a rushing sound through the air. It was followed by a dull, crashing thud in the depths of the house below—on the stone floor of the hall.

Utter silence reigned after. Nothing moved. The flame of the candle was steady. It had been steady the whole time, and the air had been undisturbed by any movement whatsoever. Palsied with terror, Aunt Julia, without waiting for her companion, began fumbling her way downstairs; she was crying gently to herself, and when Shorthouse put his arm round her and half carried her he felt that she was trembling like a leaf. He went into the little room and picked up the cloak from the floor, and, arm in arm, walking very slowly, without speaking a word or looking once behind them, they marched down the three flights into the hall.

In the hall they saw nothing, but the whole way down the stairs they were conscious that someone followed them; step by step; when they went faster IT was left behind, and when they went more slowly IT caught them up. But never once did they look behind to see; and at each turning of the staircase they lowered their eyes for fear of the following horror they might see upon the stairs above.

With trembling hands Shorthouse opened the front door, and they walked out into the moonlight and drew a deep breath of the cool night air blowing in from the sea.

Mrs Raeburn's Waxwork

Lady Eleanor Smith

The rain, which had poured with a pitiless ferocity for so long upon the chimneys and roofs of the great manufacturing city, seemed at length to enclose the whole town within towering prison walls of burnished steel. It was now afternoon; the short winter day was nearly over, and it had rained thus from dawn, would probably continue to rain throughout the night. A dark, wet dusk began to envelop the city like a sable blanket; the street lamps sprang into life, looming ahead like the ghosts of drowned and weary daffodils, casting watery and trembling reflections upon the shining rivers that were pavements. There were few people walking the mournful streets, and those that were had to struggle and batter their way through sharp gusts of wind, bent double beneath dripping and top-heavy umbrellas.

Such a one was Patrick Lamb, and so great was his hurry that more than once as he stumbled over an unperceived kerb he ran the risk of entangling both himself and his umbrella in the foaming, muddy torrents of the gutters beneath his feet. He had every reason to hurry; he was on his way to apply for a job, and he feared that unless he hastened he would be too late to secure this vacancy which meant so much to him.

Turning at last into a dark and narrow street, he saw opposite to him a ramshackle building of yellow brick, from the roof of which swelled forth a glass dome encrusted with the dirt and soot of ages. A flight of shallow steps led to a swing door. This was his destination.

He flung open the door and was immediately confronted by a turnstile, near which sat a seedy-looking man in an ill-fitting uniform not unlike that of a fireman.

'Sixpence, please,' said the man, and whistled through his teeth. Patrick Lamb shook his head.

'No...I'm not a visitor. I have an appointment with Mr Mugivan, the manager.'

'Ah—ha,' said the attendant knowingly, and showed him into a tiny slice of a room filled with papers, files, account books and dust. Here sat Mr Mugivan, a fat, podgy man with thick legs and a face like a tomato.

'Good afternoon,' said Patrick Lamb hesitatingly; 'I hear that you have a vacancy here for an—an attendant.'

Mr Mugivan stared for a moment at the young man's sallow, rather long face, at his deep-set grey eyes and slender, puny body.

'Who told you so?'

'My landlady, in Bury Street. She knew the last man you had here.' 'And what made you come?'

'Necessity. I'm in need of work. I was stranded here a week ago with a theatrical company.'

There was a silence. Mr Mugivan suddenly laughed, looking at his visitor rather defiantly with little red-rimmed eyes that were not unlike the eyes of a pig.

'Rather a come-down, isn't it, for an actor to find himself

minding Mugivan's Waxworks?'

'That doesn't matter, sir. And, if you'll only let me, I'll mind them damn well.'

'It's long hours,' said the proprietor, still speaking contemptuously. 'Nine in the morning till seven at night. An hour for lunch and an hour for tea. Two pounds a week—and the attendant has to wear a uniform. *An actor* wouldn't fancy that, would he?'

'Maybe I'm not an actor,' said Patrick Lamb.

Mr Mugivan spat upon the floor.

'I'll give you a trial, anyhow. What's your name?'

Patrick told him.

'Well, Lamb,' and the proprietor creaked himself out of his chair, revealing incidentally that he wore carpet slippers and had bunions, 'come with me and I'll show you Mugivan's Beauties before you go. You can start tomorrow morning.

Obediently Patrick followed his new employer through the turnstile, which was swung round obligingly by the other attendant, down a narrow whitewashed tunnel into a large apartment.

'Ever seen figures before?' inquired Mr Mugivan.

'Waxworks? Not since I was a lad.'

'Hall of Monarchs,' said Mr Mugivan, sucking his teeth with a deprecating sound.

The room in which they found themselves was bare and vault-like; here, too, the walls were whitewashed; the floor was covered with a red drugget, and in the middle of the room was placed a sofa upholstered in shabby crimson plush. Yet although bare the room was not empty but crowded, crowded with a pale throng of mute and stiff and silent figures. They stood in groups, a dais to each group, and were protected from the public by a red cord which imprisoned them, like sheep in a pen, so that had they wished they could not have strayed, but must forever remain captive. There they stood and would no doubt stand throughout the ages, these tinsel kings and queens, Plantagenets and Stuarts, Tudors and Hanoverians, calm and blank and dreadfully remote, pallid of check and glassy of eye, indifferent to all who passed by to gape at them—a host of waxen princes, all dead, many of them forgotten, terribly isolated in their garish splendour, uncannily galvanized into a crude semblance of life that yet denied them even the elements of life, leaving them fixed, frozen and staring, while the dust thickened upon their cheap and fusty robes of purple and sham ermine.

Opposite the door through which they had come was another door leading to yet another chamber. Mr Mugivan led the way

'Curiosities and Horrors,' he explained carelessly. They passed through the second door.

Here was another room, replica of the first, but more dimly lit, more melancholy than even the Hall of Monarchs, since the illumination that winked upon this dreary scene was greenish, ghastly; such a light as might have been expected to proceed from a sconce of corpse candles. Here were more massed ranks of still, impassive figures, paler these than the monarchs in the dim grotto of their melancholy chamber, and more repellent perhaps because their stiff, indifferent bodies were clothed in the garments of everyday and borrowed no majesty from princes' robes, however sham. A skeleton gleamed white in one corner of the room, there was a stuffed ox with six legs, a tiny waxen midget and a giant of local fame. Save for these the room was peopled only with men who had killed and who had paid the penalty for killing. A throng staring before them, expressionless, rigid, mask-like, brooding perhaps upon their cringes.

Mr Mugivan seemed more at home in the second room. He became almost conversational.

'Here's Hopkins, the Norwich strangler... Tracey, who shot a policeman... John Joseph Gilmore, cut the throats of his wife and two children...'

They moved across the room. Then, near the slit of a window, crossed by iron bars, Patrick saw her for the first time. She stood on a little dais by herself, a young woman, or, rather, the effigy of a young woman, dressed neatly in dark clothes that were already old fashioned in cut. She carried herself proudly; like a queen, and whereas the other waxworks were completely expressionless of countenance, this one alone, with proudly curling lips and short, imperious nose, seemed, he thought, actually to live, perhaps because she was disdain incarnate. She stood there easily, gracefully, long, pale hands folded upon her breast, and Patrick, gazing, felt the cool, amused stare of her grey eyes. For a moment his heart leaped sharply; startling him, and he had a sudden impulse to move forward and look more closely at her; then this sensation was succeeded by a creeping feeling of curious discomfort. He was embarrassed; he had to avert his eyes.

'Who's that woman?' he asked impetuously, and then wished that he had not spoken.

Mr Mugivan answered him casually, with his back turned to the effigy

'That's Mrs Raeburn, the poisoner...and that's the lot, so come on.'

'Mrs Raeburn? I seem to know the name.'

'No doubt, no doubt. It was well enough known at one

time.'

They walked away, towards the Hall of Monarchs, and Patrick was acutely conscious of the supercilious grey eyes that must be gazing after them. The sham eyes of a sham woman, a waxen effigy! He felt acutely ridiculous.

Mr Mugivan said no more until they found themselves once again in the little office. Then, offering Patrick a cigarette, he asked suddenly:

'You're not a fanciful sort of chap by any chance?'

'Fanciful? You mean nervous? No, I can't say that I am. Why?'

'No place for fancies, this,' confided Mr Mugivan, waving his hand in the direction of the exhibition; 'it's a lonely sort of a job most of the time, and once you start thinking the figures are looking at you, well, you're done, that's all. Last chap we had here took to having fancies. That's why you've got his job.'

Patrick felt suddenly rebellious.

'I can safely say I shan't have fancies,' he said, laughing. 'I may not be particularly brave—in fact I'm not—but I must say it would take more than a parcel of wax dolls to scare me.'

'Figures aren't dolls,' Mr Mugivan corrected, shocked.

'Figures, then,' and he thought: 'Talking of figures, that woman Mrs Raeburn's got a good one.'

But neither he nor Mr Mugivan mentioned the name of the woman poisoner aloud.

'Nine o'clock tomorrow, then,' said Mr Mugivan.

'Nine o'clock tomorrow.'

And so they parted.

He discovered, the next day two things about his new job. One was that his long and often lonely vigil with the waxworks gave him at times the curious and eerie sensation of being buried alive in a vault filled with the dead, the other that, with the morning, Mrs Raeburn, poisoner, had become once more a waxen effigy and was no longer a living, breathing woman. This was comforting, yet in some strange way disappointing, for it was idle to deny that he had thought of her very frequently during the course of the night, and that the prospect of meeting once more the direct gaze of her rather mocking eyes had undoubtedly stimulated him and sent him forth into the cheerless streets kindled with an eager, sparkling excitement which he rattler half-heartedly strove to suppress.

As the morning dragged by he studied a catalogue of the exhibition, trying to memorize the many dossiers of princes and murderers. He was accustomed to learn by heart, and in three hours his task was almost complete, yet with one exception. A curious revulsion prevented hill, from reading even to himself, the brief account in the catalogue of Mrs Raeburn's cringe, of discovering, through the medium of one cheap, smudged paragraph, that she had been an infamous woman, a monster of vice and cruelty. Taking a pen-knife from his pocket he cut away from his catalogue all record of her dark deeds. Yet she remained throughout the morning a lifeless effigy and after glancing at her once, he gladly looked away.

He went out to lunch and returned for the long vigil of the afternoon. Few people came to visit the exhibition: a pair of schoolchildren in charge of a maiden aunt, two girls, who giggled and eyed him coyly, an old mall, and all amorous couple who plainly regarded his presence as a nuisance.

It was foggy outside; dusk fell early. For the first time that day as he paced the Hall of Monarchs, he became sensible of the loneliness of his position. Once again the feeling of being buried among the dead returned to him, intensified this time by a bored and brooding melancholy whereas in the morning there had also been a sense of adventure. The very tread of his feet, the only sound in the still apartment, smote lugubriously upon his ears. He would have liked to smoke, but this was, of course, forbidden.

At length he turned, and obeying an impulse which was becoming every second stronger, he moved towards the farther chamber, the Hall of Curiosities and Horrors. Here the twilight struck gloomily upon the wan and glimmering faces of the murderers, upturned to greet the first dark, smoky greyness of night: greenish they were once more, and dismal; and very hopeless in the blank resignation of their weary vigil in this dim room that was filled with the very breath of genteel decay.

He went straight towards the figure of Mrs Raeburn, standing tall and quiet and erect on her dais below the barred window. He had never been so near to her before; their eyes met, and once more she had recaptured that spark of life which had so curiously impressed him on the previous day. He gazed for some moments at her pale, clear-cut face, at her direct, ironic eyes. She appeared to return his scrutiny gravely, earnestly; scornfully; yet with a glint of interest and humour in her regard. She seemed, he thought, a woman well used to curious eyes, well able to defend herself against the stares of the inquisitive. Suddenly; to his immense astonishment, he spoke to her, and his voice rang out strangely enough in that silent room.

'I wonder what you have done?' he asked her abruptly 'For God's sake, what can you have done that you should be here?'

There was a long pause, during the course of which he continued to examine her closely. Was it his imagination, or did her lips really curve, was there an answering twinkle in her eye? And then he turned sharply, for he had caught, or thought that he had caught, a soft, eager rustling sound from the throng of effigies behind his back. And suddenly he was saved, for two little boys came pattering in to visit the Curiosities and Horrors.

The next day saw him resolutely keeping to the Hall of Monarchs. Here, with the lifeless dummies of long dead kings, he was safe. In that other room he realized that he was in peril. And the day after, although he hungered for a glimpse of Mrs Raeburn's pale face, he still remained aloof. The next day was Saturday; with a steady stream of patrons who would have made the dankest vault seem homely and prosaic. Then Sunday, a holiday.

On Monday, he returned to the exhibition ready to laugh at himself for a morbid fool. The rain had stopped; a feeble ray of primrose sunshine, filtering through the barred window of the second chamber, made even Mrs Raeburn seem little more than a cunningly fashioned doll of life size. And he had spoken to her, as though she were alive and could hear and understand him! He was disgusted with himself.

Yet, with the swiftly flowing dusk the murderers changed once more; assumed as was their wont with the shades of night the vivid and evil personalities they must have worn during their lifetime; seemed to stretch themselves as though released from some long spell of immobility; nodded, perhaps, to one another—even winked; perhaps brushed the dust from their shabby garments, smothered yawns, and waited, quietly expectant, for the closing of the exhibition. So Patrick thought, but it was difficult to see, for the shadows were thick in this lost and forgotten room.

He went towards the effigy of Mrs Raeburn and was not surprised to find that her eyes, alive and brilliant, almost feverish in their eager intensity; remained fixed direct upon him as though she waited to see whether he would, after his three days' absence, speak once more to her.

He was, however silent. He stared at her proud and beautiful mouth, at her long, pale hands, at the white stem of her throat, and admitted to himself that he desired her. Yet he had no immediate wish to touch her, but only longed passionately for the stiff, waxen body of this effigy to melt and transform itself into warm living flesh and blood. Somewhere, somehow, this miracle must be accomplished, for if he was unable to possess her he thought that, such was the spell she had cast upon him, he must inevitably pine and sicken, for she was La Belle Dame Sans Merci, and he was in her thrall. At last he spoke to her, softly, scarcely knowing that he spoke.

'You are a witch,' he said, 'and you possess my body and soul. You ought to be burnt, and since you are made of wax it should not be difficult to destroy you... I have a good mind to try.'

This time there was no mistake; a gleam of sardonic laughter came to her eyes, a strange and elfin smile to her curling lips. She defied him. And as before, the row of murderers behind seemed to move simultaneously with the rustling murmur of excitement. As before, too, he was saved by a footstep from the outer world. He turned sharply, a woman came into the room.

Patrick stiffened, became once more the respectful and vigilant attendant. The woman hesitated for a moment, then approached him slowly; for she was bent and squat and elderly, and walked with the help of a stick. He noticed vaguely that she was dressed in dingy black, with a frowsy bonnet askew upon her head and a film of veil that partially concealed her face. He bent down politely

'Yes, madam? Is there anything I can do?'

'There is,' said the old woman. Her voice was clear and

decisive, the voice of one who is accustomed to command. 'I have stupidly neglected to buy a catalogue at the door, and as I am old, and not so good a walker as I was, I wonder if you would save my going back by being kind enough to tell me something about the waxworks. These are murderers, are they not?'

Patrick, only too pleased to occupy his mind in this accustomed fashion, began mechanically:

'Yes, madam. There on my right is Richard Sayers, the Scottish bodysnatcher, who shot two men before he was arrested, and protested his innocence to the last... Next to Sayers is Mugivan's conception of Jack the Ripper, the criminal who was never captured...this figure is modelled according to the description of his appearance given to the police by those persons who protested that they had seen hull before or after his appalling crimes... Next to Jack the Ripper we have Landru...'

But while his voice droned on he was dreading the moment when they must face Mrs Raeburn, when he would look once more upon her pale, remote face and meet once again her steady, contemptuous gaze. He lingered beside the midget, the freakish ox, the local giant. The old woman listened to him attentively, beady eyes darting from beneath her heavy veil. Once or twice she asked him a question, but otherwise was silent, seeming pleasantly absorbed in his monotonous catalogue of grim and fiendish crimes. At last the moment dreaded by Patrick could be postponed no longer; at last they faced the figure of Mrs Raeburn, standing slim and straight and self-possessed beneath the grating window. Suddenly Patrick remembered that he knew nothing of this murderess save that she had killed by poison; here he was speechless and could recite no bloodthirsty dossier, nor did he even know her victim; only that she was young and fair and that she had cast a spell upon him, and these things could not be told to his companion. There was a pause during the course of which the old woman examined the wax figure attentively and in silence. At length, he mumbled:

'This is Mrs Raeburn...the poisoner.'

As he spoke he shot a sharp glance at the effigy and observed that she was blank and mask-like once more, indifferent both to him and his companion. His witch had again become a waxwork.

The old lady shuffled closer to the figure, peered with a certain attentive inquisitiveness, then turned to him and remarked critically:

'The likeness is not very good.'

He was startled, and gaped, unable quite to grasp the purport of her words.

He asked: 'You knew her?'

She did not answer him, but said, still peering: 'She was taller, she had more dignity, more of an air. And I think she was wilder. But it's long ago,' and her face changed all the time.

He asked again, trembling, his hands clammy cold, his voice unconsciously menacing: 'You knew her?'

For the first time the old creature turned to look at him, seeming to observe him closely. She chuckled, and at first he thought that one of the waxworks had laughed, so ghostly, so unexpected, was this little bubbling sound in the quietness of the dim hall.

She said, still chuckling: 'I am Mrs Raeburn.'

And as he did not answer she pulled back her veil. She was younger than he had at first supposed. She revealed a fat, gross, heavy-jowled face, sallow, unhealthy, with high Mongolian cheekbones. Her nose was squat and thick, her cheeks carved with two deep-cut lines running from her nostrils to the corners of her mouth. Her little sharp grey eyes were almost buried in folds of flesh. Beneath the shoddy bonnet a strand of hair hung untidily; it was dyed a bright orange tint. The face, which leered forth so boldly at Patrick, was seamed and stamped with the marks of every foul and obscene vice; brazen, debauched, so brutal as to be three parts animal, it seemed to hang in the air, this gargoyle face, to gloat triumphantly upon his horror and confusion. Then, swiftly, the woman whisked back her veil and said crisply, in her clear and resonant voice: 'It didn't do me justice, your image.' Then in a moment she was gone, while behind her the effigy of Mrs Raeburn, poisoner, remained standing cool and pale and remote upon her dais, all the paler, all the cooler, for being now the centre of a flood of cold and frozen moonlight.

Patrick fled after the old woman, not because he wished to see her again, but because of the two of them the waxen image had become the more repulsive, yet, when he reached the Hall of Monarchs, she had already disappeared.

He waited, sick and shivering, until the clock struck seven and the show shut down, then he went in search of Mr Mugivan, whom he found in his office, reading an evening paper, with his feet on his desk.

'Good evening,' said Patrick. 'I want to tell you something.'

Mr Mugivan put down his paper.

'My word, young fellow, you look cheap. What is it now?'

Patrick, gulping, said: 'Do you know who's been here this afternoon?'

'I do not,' said Mr Mugivan. 'I'm proprietor of a waxwork show, not a magician. Who has been here?'

'Mrs Raeburn. The real Mrs Raeburn. She came to see her waxwork. She's just gone.'

As Mr Mugivan gaped, his red face became curiously mottledwhite and purple in patches, Patrick noticed dispassionately 'Mrs Raeburn?'

'Yes.'

Mr Mugivan climbed laboriously from his chair.

'Mrs Raeburn, eh? Somebody's been pulling your leg. You don't know your catalogue, either. Mrs Raeburn indeed?'

And he pulled a document from the untidy desk, licked his thumb, and flipped over a page.

'Mrs Raeburn,' he said, speaking very loud and not looking at Patrick, 'was scragged—hanged, you understand—hanged by the neck for the murder of her husband more than twenty years ago. That being so, you could hardly have seen her here just now. And that's enough of your funny stuff for one day.'

Patrick said nothing. There was really nothing to say nor did Mr Mugivan break the silence, but waddled to and fro about the little room, changing his carpet slippers for boots, struggling into his overcoat, cramming a check cap upon his head. In a moment he had gone.

Patrick switched off the office light, then went forth, as was his custom, to extinguish the gas jets in the exhibition before locking up for the night. His comrade of the turnstile had already gone home; he was alone, entirely alone, with more than a hundred waxen effigies. It was now quite dark outside, for the moon had fled behind a screen of clouds, and there was a rushing sound of strong wind, which swept in gusts past the shuttered windows.

He paused to light a forbidden cigarette, and then it was that he realized with an odd detachment that what he had seen during the afternoon was not a ghost, but something even more monstrous—a disembodied soul. The foul and evil soul of this wretched woman whose lovely image had bewitched him. The hideous reflection of a hideous mind. Behind her seeming purity and beauty had always been this horror, dormant, waiting to leap forth and devour. The wind rose, moaning, battering at the panes.

On such a night, he mused, as he tramped towards the Monarchs, ghouls would surely stalk abroad and witches soar through the air clutching their broomsticks and screaming aloud their lust for satan, vampires, sorcerers and fiends. A nightmare pack of horrors... He stretched on tiptoe to lower the gas above the wan, impassive face of King Richard II... And in the old days witches were burnt alive like the guys now consumed by flames each Fifth of November... And after burning he supposed that these evil women could do no more harm, but were destroyed forever, they and their spells. A good job, too. He entered the second chamber.

◆

That night the inhabitants of the city were surprised to perceive a crimson flush sweeping the sky above the roof tops of a distant street. Then came a clanging of bells, a roar of motor-engines, and, hot-toot, in pursuit of the fire brigade, a yelling, excited rabble. Mugivan's Waxwork Exhibition was on tire. No one wanted to miss the show, doubly welcome because it was free.

The wind was strong that night, and licked the flames eagerly, strengthening them until the efforts of the men armed with hosepipes became pathetic in their futility. At length the roof crashed in, and a wall of roaring flame rose as though to leap into the sky. They were triumphant, these pillars of tire, as though they knew that they were purifying, destroying a witch.

By morning Mugivan's Waxwork Show was a drenched

and sooty ruin. Many of the figures were entirely destroyed, the Monarchs having been on the whole unluckier than the Murderers. Down in the Hall of Curiosities and Horrors there were a few survivors. Some were quite untouched. Mrs Raeburn, for instance, appeared to have emerged unscathed from the ordeal, and stood upon her dais proudly and gracefully, pale hands folded demurely upon her breast. And yet, on closer inspection, Mrs Raeburn proved not to be entirely unharmed.

Her waxen face had melted, and running, the stuff had twisted upon her features a strange and devilish sneer. Save for her pride of carriage she was unrecognizable, distorted. And then the firemen made a further discovery.

Lying near by, where the flames had crackled most fiercely was a charred and sodden bundle of clothing. They bent to examine it. It was, they found, a human body, the body of a young man.

Football On The Tung—T'ing Lake
(China)

Herbert A. Miles

Wang Shih-hsiu was a native of Lu-chou, and such a strong fellow that he could pick up a stone mortar. Father and son were both good football players; but when the former was about forty years of age he was drowned while crossing the Money Pool. Eight or nine years later our hero happened to be on his way of Hunan; and anchoring in the Tung—t'ing lake, watched the moon rising in the east and illuminating the water into a bright sheet of light. While he was thus engaged, lo! from out of the lake emerged five men, bringing with them a large mat, which they spread on the surface of the water so as to cover about six yards square. Wine and food were then arranged upon it, and Wang heard the sound of the dishes knocking together, but it was a dull, soft sound, not at all that of ordinary crockery. Three of the men sat on the mat and the other two waited upon them. One of the former was dressed in yellow, the other two in white, and each wore a black turban. Their demeanour, as they sat there side by side, was grave and dignified; in appearance they resembled three of the ancients, but by the fitful beams of the moon Wang was unable to see very clearly what they were like. The attendants wore black serge dresses, and one of them seemed to be a boy, while the other was many years older. Wang now heard the man in the yellow dress say, 'This is truly a fine moonlight night for a drinking bout;' to which one of his companions replied, 'It quite reminds me of the night when Prince Kuang-li feasted at Pear-blossom Island.' The three then pledged each other in clinking goblets, talking all the time in such a low tone that Wang could not hear what they were saying. The boatmen kept themselves concealed, crouching down at the bottom of the boat; but Wang looked hard at the attendants, the elder of whom bore a striking resemblance to his father, though he spoke in quite a different tone of voice. When it was drawing towards midnight, one of them proposed a game at ball; and in a moment the boy disappeared into the water, to return immediately with a huge ball—quite an armful in fact—apparently full of quicksilver, and lustrous within and without. All now rose, and the man in the yellow dress bade the old attendant join them in the game. The ball was kicked up about ten or fifteen feet in the air, and was quite dazzling in its brilliancy; but once, when it had gone up with a whish—h—h, it fell at some distance off, right in the very middle of Wang's boat. The occasion was irresistible, and Wang, exerting all his strength, kicked the ball with all his might. It seemed unusually light and soft to the touch, and his foot broke right through. Away went the ball to a good height, pouring forth a stream of light like a rainbow from the hole Wang had made, and making as it fell, a curve like that of a comet rushing across the sky. Down it glided into the water, where it fizzed a moment and then went out. 'Ho there!' cried out the players in anger, 'what living creature is that who dares thus to interrupt our sport?' 'Well kicked indeed!' said the old man, 'that's a favourite dropkick of my own.' At this, one of the two in white clothes began to abuse him, saying, 'What! You old baggage, when we are all so annoyed in this manner, are you to come forward and make a joke of it? Go at once with the boy and bring back to us this practical joker, or your own back will have a taste of the stick.' Wang was of course unable to flee; however, he was not a bit afraid, and grasping a sword stood there in the middle of the boat. In a moment, the old man and boy arrived, also armed, and then Wang knew that the former was really his father, and called out to him at once. 'Father, I am your son.' The old man was greatly alarmed, but father and son forgot their troubles in the joy of meeting once again. Meanwhile, the boy went back, and Wang's father bade him hide, or they would all be lost. The words were hardly out of his mouth when the three men jumped on board the boat. Their faces were black as pitch, their eyes as big as pomegranates, and they at once proceeded to seize the old man. Wang struggled hard with them, and managing to get the boat free from her moorings, he seized his sword and cut off one of his adversaries' arms. The arm dropped and the man in the yellow dress ran away; whereupon one of those in white rushed at Wang, who immediately cut off his head, and he fell into the water with a splash, at which the third disappeared. Wang and his father were now anxious to get away, when suddenly a great mouth arose from the lake, as big and deep as a well, and against which they could hear the noise of the water when it struck. This mouth blew forth a violent gust of wind, and in a moment the waves were mountains high and all the boats on the lake were tossing about. The boatmen were terrified, but Wang seized one of two huge stones there were on board for use as anchors, about 130 lb. in weight, and threw it into the water, which immediately began to subside; and then he threw in the other one, upon which the wind dropped, and the lake became calm again. Wang thought his father was a disembodied spirit, but the old man said, 'I never died. There were nineteen of us drowned in the river; all of whom were eaten by the fish-goblins except myself: I was saved because I could play football. Those you saw got into trouble with the Dragon King, and were sent here. They were all marine creatures, and the ball they were playing with was a fish-bladder.' Father and son were overjoyed at meeting again, and at once proceeded on their way. In the morning, they found in the boat a huge fin—the arm that Wang had cut off the night before.

The Isle of Voices
(Hawaii)

R.L. Stevenson

Keola was married to Lehua, daughter of Kalamake, the wise man of Molokai, and he kept his dwelling with the father of his wife. There was no man more cunning than that prophet; he read the stars, he could divine by the bodies of the dead, and by means of evil creatures: he could go alone into the highest parts of the mountain, into the region of the hobgoblins, and there he would lay snares to entrap the spirits of the ancient. For this reason no man was more consulted in all the kingdom of Hawaii. Prudent people bought, and sold, and married, and laid out their lives by his counsels; and the King had him sent twice to Kona to seek the treasures of Kamehameha. Neither was any man more feared: of his enemies, some had dwindled in sickness by the virtue of his incantations, and some had been spirited away, the life and the clay both, so that folk looked in vain for so much as a bone of their bodies. It was rumoured that he had the art or the gift of the old heroes. Men had seen him at night upon the mountains, stepping from one cliff to the next; they had seen him walking in the high forest, and his head and shoulders were above the trees.

This Kalamake was a strange man to look at. He came of the best blood in Molokai and Maui, of a pure descent; and yet he was more white to look upon than any foreigner; his hair the colour of dry grass, and his eyes red and very blind, so that 'Blind as Kalamake that can see across tomorrow,' was a byword in the islands.

Of all these doings of his father-in-law, Keola knew a little by common repute, a little more he suspected, and the rest he ignored. But there was one thing that troubled him. Kalamake was a man that spared for nothing, whether to eat or to drink, or to wear; and for all he paid in bright new dollars. 'Bright as Kalamake's dollars,' was another saying in the Eight Isles. Yet he neither sold, nor planted, nor hired—only now and then for his sorceries—and there was no source conceivable for so much silver.

It chanced one day, Keola's wife was gone upon a visit to Kaunakakai on the lee side of the island, and the men were at the sea, fishing. But Keola was an idle clog, and he lay in the verandah and watched the surf heat on the shore and the birds fly about the cliff. It was the chief thought with him always—the thought of the bright dollars. When he lay down to bed he would be wondering why they were so many, and when he woke at morn he would be wondering why they were all new; and the thing was never absent from his mind. But this day of all days he resolved of some discovery.

For he had observed the place where Kalamake kept his treasure, which was a lockfast desk against the parlour wall, under the print of Kamehameha the Fifth, and a photograph of Queen Victoria with her crown; and no later than the night before, he found occasion to look in, and behold! the bag lay there empty. And this was the day of the steamer; he could see her smoke off Kalaupapa; and she must soon arrive with a month's goods, tinned salmon and gin, and all manner of rare luxuries for Kalamake.

'Now if he can pay for his goods today,' Keola thought, 'I shall know for certain that the man is a warlock, and the dollars come out of the devil's pocket.'

While he was so thinking, there was his father-in-law behind him, looking vexed.

'Is that the steamer?' he asked.

'Yes,' said Keola. 'She has but to call at Pelekunu, and then she will be here.'

'There is no help for it then,' returned Kalamake, 'and I must take you in my confidence, Keola, for the lack of anyone better. Come here within the house.'

So they stepped together into the parlour, which was a very fine room, papered and hung with prints, and furnished with a rocking chair, and a table and a sofa in the European style. There was a shelf of books beside, and a family Bible in the midst of the table, and the lockfast writing desk against the wall; so that any one could see it was the house of a man of substance.

Kalamake made Keola close the shutters of the windows, while he himself locked all the doors and set open the lid of the desk. From this he brought forth a pair of necklaces hung with charms and shells, a bundle of dried herbs, and the dried leaves of trees, and a green palm branch.

'What I am about,' said he, 'is a thing beyond wonder. The men of old were wise; they wrought marvels, and this among the rest; but that was at night, in the dark, under fit stars and in the desert. The same will I do here in my own house, and under the plain eye of day.' So saying, he put the Bible under the cushion of the sofa so that it was all covered, brought out from the same place a mat of a wonderfully fine texture, and heaped the herbs and leaves on sand in a tin pan. And then he and Keola put on the necklaces, and took their stand upon the opposite corners of the mat.

'The time comes,' said the warlock, 'be not afraid.'

With that he set flame to the herbs, and began to mutter and wave the palm. At first the light was dim because of the closed shutters; but the herbs caught strongly afire, and the Haines beat upon Keola, and the room glowed with the burning; and next the smoke rose and made his head swim and his eyes darken, and the sound of Kalamake muttering ran in his cars. And suddenly, to the mat on which they were standing came a snatch or twitch, that seemed to he more swift than lightning. In the same wink the room was gone, and the house, the breath all beaten from Keola's body. Volumes of sun rolled upon his eyes and head, and he found himself transported to a beach, under a strong sun, with a great surf roaring: he and the warlock standing there on the same mat, speechless, gasping, and grasping at one another, and passing their hands before their eyes.

'What was this?' cried Keola, who came to himself the first, because he was the younger. 'The pang of it was like death.'

'It matters not,' panted Kalamake. 'It is now done.'

'And, in the name of God, where are we?' cried Keola.

'That is not the question,' replied the sorcerer. 'Being here, we have a matter that we must attend to. Go, while I recover my breath, into the borders of the wood, and bring me the leaves of such and such a herb, and such and such a tree, which you will find to grow there plentifully—three handfuls of each. And be speedy. We must be home again before the steamer conies; it would seem strange if we had disappeared.' And he sat on the sand and panted.

Keola went up the beach, which was of shining sand and coral, strewn with singular shells; and he thought in his heart:

'How do I not know this beach? I will come here again and gather shells.'

In front of him was a line of palms against the sky; not like the palms of the Eight Islands, but tall and fresh and beautiful, and hanging out withered fans like gold among the green, and he thought in his heart:

'It is strange I should not have found this grove. I will come here again, when it is warm, to sleep.' And he thought, 'How warm it has grown suddenly!' For it was winter in Hawaii, and the day had been chilly. And he thought also, 'Where are the grey mountains? And where is the high cliff with the hanging forest and the wheeling birds?' And the more he considered, the less he could conceive in what quarter of the islands he was fallen.

In the border of the grove, where it met the beach, the herb was growing, but the tree farther back. Now, as Keola went towards the tree, he was aware of a young woman who had nothing on her body but a belt of leaves.

'Well!' thought Keola, 'they are not very particular about their dress in this part of the country.' And he paused, supposing she would observe him and escape; and seeing that she still looked before her, stood and hummed aloud. Up she leaped at the sound. Her race was ashen; she looked this way and that, and her mouth gaped with the terror of her soul. But it was a strange thing that her eyes did not rest upon Keola.

'Good day,' said he. 'You need not be so frightened, I will not eat you.' And he had scarce opened his mouth before the young woman fled into the bush.

'These are strange manners,' thought Keola, and, not thinking what he did, ran after her.

As she ran, the girl kept crying in some speech that was not practised in Hawaii, yet some of the words were the same, and he knew she kept calling and warning others. And presently he saw more people running—men, women, and children, one with another, all running and crying like people at a fire. And with that he began to grow afraid himself, and returned to Kalamake bringing the leaves. Him he told what he had seen.

'You must pay no heed,' said Kalamake. All this is like a dream and shadows. All will disappear and be forgotten.'

'It seemed none saw me,' said Keola.

'And none did,' replied the sorcerer. 'We walk here in the broad sun invisible by reason of these charms. Yet they hear us; and therefore it is well to speak softly, as I do.'

With that he made a circle round the mat with stones, and in the midst he set the leaves.

'It will be your part,' said he, 'to keep the leaves alight, and feed the fire slowly. While they blaze (which is but for a little moment) I must do my errand; and before the ashes blacken, the same power that brought us carries us away. Be ready now with the match; and call me in good time lest the flames burn out and I be left.'

As soon as the leaves caught, the sorcerer leaped like a deer out of the circle, and began to race along the beach like a hound that has been bathing. As he ran, he kept stooping to snatch shells; and it seemed to Keola that they glittered as he took them. The leaves blazed with a clear flame that consumed them swiftly; and presently Keola had but a handful left, and the sorcerer was far off, running and stopping.

'Back!' cried Keola. 'Back! The leaves are nearly done.'

At that Kalamake turned, and if he had run before, now he flew. But fast as he ran, the leaves burned faster. The flame was ready to expire when, with a great leap, he bounded on the mat. The wind of his leaping blew it out; and with that the beach was gone, and the sun and the sea; and they stood once more in the dimness of the shuttered parlour, and were once more shaken and blinded; and on the mat betwixt them lay a pile of shining dollars. Keola ran to the shutters; and there was the steamer tossing in the swell close in.

The same night Kalamake took his son-in-law apart, and gave him five dollars in his hand.

'Keola,' said he, 'if you are a wise man (which I am doubtful of) you will think you slept this afternoon on the verandah, and dreamed as you were sleeping. I am a man of few words, and I have for my helpers people of short memories.'

Never a word more said Kalamake, nor referred again to that affair. But it ran all the while in Keola's head—if he were lazy before, he would now do nothing.

'Why should I work,' thought he, 'when I have a father-in-law who makes dollars of seashells?'

Presently his share was spent. He spent it all upon fine clothes. And then he was sorry:

'For,' thought he, 'I had done better to have bought a concertina, with which I might have entertained myself all clay long.' And then he began to grow vexed with Kalamake.

'This man has the soul of a dog,' thought he. 'He can gather dollars when he pleases on the beach, and he leaves me to pine for a concertina! Let him beware: I am no child, I am as cunning as he, and hold his secret.' With that he spoke to his wife Lehua, and complained of her father's manners.

'I would let my father be,' said Lehua. 'He is a dangerous man to cross.'

'I care not for him!' cried Keola; and snapped his fingers. 'I have him by the nose. I can make him do what I please.' And he told Lehua the story.

But she shook her head.

'You may do what you like,' said she; 'but as sure as you thwart my father, you will be no more heard of. Think of this person, and that person; think of Hua, who was a noble of the House of Representatives, and went to Honolulu every year; and not a bone or a hair of him was found. Remember Kamau, and how he wasted to a thread, so that his wife lifted him with one hand. Keola, you are a baby in my father's hands; he will take you with his thumb and finger and eat you like a shrimp.'

Now Keola was truly afraid of Kalamake, but he was vain too; and these words incensed him.

'Very well,' said he, 'if that is what you think of me, I will show how much you are deceived.' And he went straight to where his father-in-law was sitting in the parlour.

'Kalamake,' said he, 'I want a concertina.'

'Do you, indeed?' said Kalamake.

'Yes,' said he, 'and I may as well tell you plainly, I mean to have it. A man who picks up dollars on the beach can certainly afford a concertina.'

'I had no idea you had so much spirit,' replied the sorcerer. 'I thought you were a timid, useless lad, and I cannot describe how much pleased I am to find I was mistaken. Now I begin to think I may have found an assistant and successor in my difficult business. A concertina? You shall have the best in Honolulu. And tonight, as soon as it is dark, you and I will go and find the money.'

'Shall we return to the beach?' asked Keola.

'No, no!' replied Kalamake; 'you must begin to learn more of my secrets. Last time I taught you to pick shells; this time I shall teach you to catch fish. Are you strong enough to launch Pili's boat?'

'I think I am,' returned Keola. 'But why should we not take your own, which is afloat already?'

'I have a reason which you will understand thoroughly before tomorrow,' said Kalamake. 'Pili's boat is the better suited for my purpose. So, if you please, let us meet there as soon as it is dark; and in the meanwhile, let us keep our own counsel, for there is no cause to let the family into our business.'

Honey is not more sweet than was the voice of Kalamake, and Keola could scarce contain his satisfaction.

'I might have had my concertina weeks ago,' thought he, 'and there is nothing needed in this world but a little courage.'

Presently after he spied Lehua weeping, and was half in a mind to tell her all was well.

'But no,' thinks he; 'I shall wait until I can show her the concertina; we shall see what the chit will do then. Perhaps she will understand in the future that her husband is a man of some intelligence.'

As soon as it was dark, father and son-in-law launched Pili's boat and set the sail. There was a great sea, and it blew strong from the leeward; but the boat was swift and light and dry, and skimmed the waves. The wizard had a lantern, which he lit and held with his finger through the ring; and the two sat in the stern and smoked cigars, of which Kalamake always had a provision, and spoke like friends of magic and the great sums of money which they could make by its exercise, and what they should buy first, and what second; and Kalamake talked like a father.

Presently he looked all about, and above him at the stars, and back at the island, which was already three parts sunk under the sea, and he seemed to consider ripely his position.

'Look!' says he, 'There is Molokai already far behind us, and Maui like a cloud; and by the bearing of these three stars I know I am come to where I desire. This part of the sea is called the Sea of the Dead. It is in this place extraordinarily deep, and the floor is all covered with the bones of men, and in the holes of this part gods and goblins keep their habitation. The flow of the sea is to the north, stronger than a shark can swim, and any man who shall here be thrown out of a ship, it bears away like a wild horse into the uttermost ocean. Presently he is spent and goes down, and his bones are scattered with the rest, and the gods devour his spirit.'

Fear came on Keola at the words, and he looked, and by the light of the stars and the lantern, the warlock seemed to change.

'What ails you?' cried Keola, quick and sharp.

'It is not I who am ailing,' said the wizard; 'but there is one here very sick.'

With that he changed his grasp upon the lantern, and, behold—as he drew his finger from the ring, the finger stuck and the ring was burst, and his hand was grown to be the bigness of three.

At that sight Keola screamed and covered his face.

But Kalamake held up the lantern.

'Look rather at my face!' said he—and his head was huge as a barrel; and still he grew and grew as a cloud grows on a mountain, and Keola sat before him screaming, and the boat raced on the great seas.

'And now,' said the wizard, 'what do you think about that concertina? Are you sure you would not rather have a flute?

No?' says he; 'that is well, for I do not like my family to be changeable of purpose. But I begin to think I had better get out of this paltry boat, for my bulk swells to a very unusual degree, and if we are not the more careful, she will presently be swamped.'

With that he threw his legs over the side. Even as he did so, the greatness of the man grew thirtyfold and fortyfold as swift as sight or thinking, so that he stood in the deep seas to the armpits, and his head and shoulders rose like a high isle, and the swell beat and burst upon his bosom, as it beats and breaks against a cliff. The boat ran still to the north, but he reached out his hand, and took the gunwale by the finger and thumb, and broke the side like a biscuit, and Keola was spilled into the sea. And the pieces of the boat the sorcerer crushed in the hollow of his hand and flung miles away into the night.

'Excuse me for taking the lantern,' said he; 'for I have a long wade before me, and the land is far, and the bottom of the sea uneven, and I feel the bones under my toes.'

And he turned and went off walking with great strides; and as often as Keola sank in the trough he could see him no longer; but as often as he was heaved upon the crest, there he was striding and dwindling, and he held the lamp high over his head, and the waves broke white about him as he went.

Since first the islands were fished out of the sea, there was never a man so terrified as Keola. He swam indeed, but he swam as puppies swim when they are cast in to drown, and knew not wherefore. He could but think of the hugeness of the swelling of the warlock, of that face which was great as a mountain, of those shoulders that were broad as an isle, and of the seas that beat on them in vain. He thought, too, of the concertina, and shame took hold upon him; and of the dead men's bones, and fear shook him.

Of a sudden he was aware of something dark against the stars that tossed, and a light below, and a brightness of the cloven sea; and he heard the speech of men. He cried out loud and a voice answered; and in a twinkling the bows of a ship hung above him on a wave like a thing balanced, and swooped down. He caught with his two hands in the chains of her, and the next moment was buried in the rushing seas, and the next hauled on hoard by seamen.

They gave him gin and biscuits and dry clothes, and asked him how he came where they found him, and whether the light which they had seen was the lighthouse, Lae o Ka Laau. But Keola knew white men are like children and only believe their own stories; so about himself he told them what he pleased, and as for the light (which was Kalamake's lantern) he vowed he had seen none.

This ship was a schooner bound for Honolulu, and then to trade in the low islands; and by a very good chance for Keola she had lost a man off the bowsprit in a squall. Keola dared not stay in the Eight Islands. Word goes round so quickly, and all men are so fond to talk and carry news, that if he hid in the north end of Kauai or in the south end of Kau, the wizard would have wind of it before a month, and he must perish. So he did what seemed the most prudent, and shipped sailor in place of the man who had been drowned.

In some ways the ship was a good place. The food was extraordinarily rich and plenty, with biscuits and salt beef every day, and pea soup and puddings made of flour and suet twice a week, so that Keola grew fat. The captain also was a good man, and the crew no worse. The trouble was the mate, who was the most difficult man to please, and who beat and cursed him daily, both for what he did and what he did not. The blows that he dealt were very sure, for he was strong; and the words he used were very unpalatable, for Keola was come of a good family and accustomed to respect. And what was the worst of all, whenever Keola found a chance to sleep, there was the mate awake and stirring him up with a rope's end. Keola saw it would never do; and he made up his mind to run away.

They were about a month out from Honolulu when they made land. It was a fine starry night, the sea was smooth as well as the sky fair; it blew a steady trade; and there was the island on their weather bow, a ribbon of palm trees lying flat along the sea. The captain and the mate looked at it with the night glass, and named the name of it, and talked of it, beside the wheel where Keola was steering. It seemed it was an isle where no traders came. By the captain's way, it was an isle besides where no man dwelt; but the mate thought otherwise.

'I don't give a cent for the directory,' said he. 'I've been past here one night in the schooner *Eugenie,* it was just such a night as this; they were fishing with torches, and the beach was thick with lights like a town.'

'Well, well,' says the captain, 'it's steep-to, that's the great point; and there ain't any outlying dangers, by the chart, so we'll just hug the lee side of it. Keep her ramping full, don't I tell you!' he cried to Keola, who was listening so hard that he forgot to steer.

And the mate cursed him, and swore that Kanaka was for no use in the world, and if he got started after him with a belaying pin, it would be a cold day for Keola.

And so the captain and mate lay down on the house together, and Keola was left to himself.

'This island will do very well for me,' he thought; 'if

no traders deal there, the mate will never come. And as for Kalamake, it is not possible he can ever get as far as this.'

With that he kept edging the schooner nearer in. He had to do this quietly, for it was the trouble with these men, and above all with the mate, that you could never be sure of them; they would all be sleeping sound, or else pretending, and if a sail shook, they would jump to their feet and fall on you with a rope's end. So Keola edged her up little by little, and kept all drawing. And presently the land was close on board, and the sound of the sea on the sides of it grew loud.

With that, the mate sat up suddenly upon the house.

'What are you doing?' he roars. 'You'll have the ship ashore!'

And he made one bound for Keola, and Keola made another clean over the rail and plump into the starry sea. When he came up again, the schooner had payed off on her true course, and the mate stood by the wheel himself and Keola heard him cursing. The sea was smooth under the lee of the island; it was warm besides, and Keola had his sailor's knife, so he had no fear of sharks. A little way before him the trees stopped; there was a break in the line of the land like the mouth of a harbour; and the tide, which was then flowing, took him up and carried him through. One minute he was without, and the next within, he floated there in wide shallow water, bright with ten thousand stars, and all about him was the ring of the land with its string of palm trees. And he was amazed, because this was a kind of island he had never heard of.

At first he sought everywhere and found no man; only some houses standing in a hamlet, and the marks of fires. But the ashes of the fires were cold and the rains had washed them away; and the winds had blown, and some of the huts were overthrown. It was here he took his dwelling; and he made a fire drill, and a shell hook, and fished and cooked his fish, and climbed after green cocoa nuts, the juice of which he drank, for in all the isle there was no water. The days were long to him, and the nights terrifying. He made a lamp of cocoa shell, and drew the oil off the ripe nuts, and made a wick of fibre; and when evening came he closed up his hut, and lit his lamp, and lay and trembled until morning. Many a time he thought in his heart he would have been better off in the bottom of the sea, his bones rolling there with the others.

All this while he kept by the inside of the island, for the huts were on the shore of the lagoon, and it was there the palms grew best, and the lagoon itself abounded with good fish. And to the outer side he went once only, and he looked but once at the beach of the ocean, and came away shaking. For the look of it, with its bright sand, and strewn shells, and strong sun and surf, went sore against his inclination.

'It cannot be,' he thought, 'and yet it is very like. And how do I know? These white men, although they pretend to know where they are sailing, must take their chance like other people. So that after all, we may have sailed in a circle, and I may be quite near to Molokai, and this may be the very beach where my father-in-law gathers his dollars.'

So after that he was prudent, and kept to the land side.

It was perhaps a month later, when the people of the place arrived—filling six great boats. They were a fine race of men, and spoke a tongue that sounded very different from the tongue of Hawaii, but so many of the words were the same that it was not difficult to understand. The men besides were very courteous, and the women very towardly; and they made Keola welcome, and built him a house, and gave him a wife; and what surprised him the most, he was never sent to work with the young men.

A cause of alarm for him was his wife. He was in doubt about the island, and he might have been in doubt about the speech, of which he had heard so little when he came there with the wizard. But about his wife there was no mistake conceivable, for she was the same girl that ran from him crying in the wood. So he had sailed all this way, and might as well have stayed in Molokai; he had left home and his wife and all his friends for no other cause but to escape his enemy, and the place he had come to was that wizard's hunting ground, the place where he had walked invisible. It was at this period when he kept the most close to the lagoon side, and, as far as he dared, in the cover of his hut.

The second cause of alarm was talk he had heard from his wife and the chief islanders. Keola himself said little. He was never so sure of his new friends, for he judged they were too civil to be wholesome, and since he had grown better acquainted with his father-in-law, the man had grown more cautious. So he told them nothing of himself, but only his name and descent, and that he came from the Eight Islands, and what fine islands they were; and about the king's palace in Honolulu, and how he was a chief friend of the king and the missionaries. But he put out many questions and learned much. The island where he was, was called the Isle of Voices; it belonged to the tribe, but they made their home upon another, three hours' sail to the southward. There they lived and had their permanent houses, and it was a rich island, where there were eggs and chickens and pigs, and ships came trading with rum and tobacco. It was there the schooner had gone after Keola deserted; there, too, the mate had died, like the fool of a man as he was. It seems, when the ship came, it was the beginning of the sickly season in that isle, when the fish of the lagoon are poisonous, and all who eat of them swell up and die. The mate was told of it; he saw the boats preparing, because in that season the people leave that island and sail to the Isle of Voices; but he was a fool of a white man, who would believe no stories but his own, and he caught one of these fish, cooked it and ate it, and swelled up and died, which was good news to Keola. As for the Isle of Voices, it lay solitary the most part of the year, only now and then a boat's crew came for copra, and in the bad season, when the fish at the main isle were poisonous, the tribe dwelt there in a body. It had its name from a marvel, for it seemed the sea side of it was all beset with invisible devils; day and night you heard them talking with one another in strange tongues; day and night little fires blazed tip and were extinguished on the beach; and what was the cause of these doings no man might conceive. Keola asked them if it were the same in their own island where they stayed, and they told him no, not there; nor yet in any other of the hundred isles that lay all about them in that sea; but it was a thing peculiar to the Isle of Voices. They told him also that these fires and voices were ever on the sea side and in the seaward fringes of the wood, and a man might dwell by the lagoon two thousand years (if he could live so long) and never be in any way troubled; and even on the seaside the devils did no harm if left alone. Only once a chief had cast a spear at one of the voices, and the same night he fell out of a cocoa nut palm and was killed.

Keola thought a good bit. He saw he would be all right when the tribe returned to the main island, and right enough where he was, if he kept by the lagoon, yet he had a mind to make things righter if he could. So he told the high chief he had once been in an isle that was pestered the same way, and the folk had found a means to cure that trouble.

'There was a tree growing in the bush there,' says he, 'and it seems these devils came to get the leaves of it. So the people of the isle cut down the tree wherever it was found, and the devils came no more.'

They asked what kind of a tree this was, and he showed them the tree of which Kalamake burned the leaves. They found it hard to believe, yet the idea tickled them. Night after night the old men debated it in their councils, but the high chief (though he was a brave man) was afraid of the matter, and reminded them daily of the chief who cast a spear against the voices and was killed, and the thought of that brought all to a stand again.

Though he could not yet bring about the destruction of the trees, Keola was well pleased, and began to look about him and take pleasure in his days; and, among other things, he was kinder to his wife, so that the girl began to love him greatly. One day he came to the hut, and she lay on the ground lamenting.

'Why,' said Keola, 'what is wrong with you now?' She declared it was nothing.

The same night she woke him. The lamp burned very low, but he saw by her face she was in sorrow.

'Keola,' she said, 'put your ear to my mouth that I may whisper, for no one must hear us. Two days before the boats begin to be got ready, go you to the seaside of the isle and lie in a thicket. We shall choose that place beforehand, you and I; and hide food; and every night I shall come near by there singing. So when a night comes and you do not hear me, you shall know we are clean gone out of the island, and you may come forth again in safety.'

The soul of Keola died within him.

'What is this?' he cried. 'I cannot live among devils. I will not be left behind upon this isle, I am dying to leave it.'

'You will never leave it alive, my poor Keola,' said the girl; 'for to tell you the truth, my people are eaters of men; but this they keep secret. And the reason they will kill you before we leave is because in our island ships come, and Donat-Kimaran comes and talks for the French, and there is a white trader there in a house with a verandah, and a catechist. Oh, that is a fine place indeed! The trader has barrels filled with flour; and a French warship once came in the lagoon and gave everybody wine and biscuit. Ah, my poor Keola, I wish I could take you there, for great is my love to you, and it is the finest place in the seas except Papeete.'

Now Keola was the most terrified man in the four oceans. He had heard tales of eaters of men in the south islands, and the thing had always been a fear to him; and here it was knocking at his door. He had heard besides, by travellers, of their practices, and how when they are in a mind to eat a man, they cherish and fondle him like a mother with a favourite baby. And he saw this must be his own case; and that was why he had been housed, and fed, and wived, and liberated from all work; and why the old men and the chiefs discoursed with him like a person of weight. So he lay on his bed and railed upon his destiny; and the flesh curdled on his bones.

The next day the people of the tribe were very civil, as their way was. They were elegant speakers, and they made beautiful poetry, and jested at meals, so that a missionary must have died laughing. It was little enough Keola cared for their fine ways; all he saw were the white teeth shining in their mouths, and his gorge rose at the sight; and when they were done eating, he went and lay in the bush like a dead man.

The next day it was the same, and then his wife followed him.

'Keola,' she said, 'if you do not eat, I tell you plainly you will be killed and cooked tomorrow Some of the old chiefs are murmuring already. They think you are fallen sick and must lose flesh.'

With that Keola got to his feet, and anger burned in him. 'It is little I care one way or the other,' said he. 'I am between the devil and the deep sea. Since die I must, let me die the quickest way; and since I must be eaten at the best of it, let me rather be eaten by hobgoblins than by men. Farewell,' said he, and he left her standing, and walked to the sea side of that island.

It was all bare in the strong sun; there was no sign of man, only the beach was trodden, and all about him as he went, the voices talked and whispered, and the little fires sprang up and burned down. All tongues of the earth were spoken there: French, Dutch, Russian, Tamil, Chinese. Whatever land knew sorcery, there were some of its people whispering in Keola's ear. That beach was thick as a fair, yet no man seen; and as he walked he saw the shells vanish before him, and no man to pick them up. I think the devil would have been afraid to be alone in such company; but Keola was past fear and courted death. When the fires sprang up, he charged for them like a bull. Bodiless voices called to and fro; unseen hands poured sand upon the flames; and they were gone from the beach before he reached them.

'It is plain Kalamake is not here,' he thought, 'or I must have been killed long since.'

With that he sat him down in the margin of the wood, for he was tired, and put his chin upon his hands. The business before his eyes continued; the beach babbled with voices, and the fires sprang up and sank, and the shells vanished and were renewed again even while he looked.

'It was a by-day when I was here before,' he thought, 'for it was nothing to this.'

And his head was dizzy with the thought of these millions and millions of dollars, and all these hundreds and hundreds of persons culling them upon the beach, and flying in the air higher and swifter than eagles.

And to think how they have fooled me with their talk of mints,' says he, 'and that money was made there, when it is clear that all the new coins in all the world is gathered on these sands! But I will know better the next time!' said he.

And at last, he knew not very well how or when, sleep fell on Keola, and he forgot the island and all his sorrow.

Early the next day, before the sun was yet up, a bustle woke him. He awoke in fear, for he thought the tribe had caught him napping; but it was no such matter. Only, on the beach in front of him, the bodiless voices called and shouted one upon another, and it seemed they all passed and swept beside him up the coast of the island.

'What is afoot now?' thinks Keola. And it was plain to him it was something beyond ordinary, for the fires were not lit nor the shells taken, but the bodiless voices kept posting up the beach, and hailing and dying away; and others following, and by the sound of them these wizards should be angry.

'It is not me they are angry at,' thought Keola, 'for they pass me close.'

As when hounds go by, or horses in a race, or city folk coursing to a fire, and all men join and follow after, so it was now with Keola; and he knew not what he did, nor why he did it, but there, lo and behold! he was running with the voices.

So he turned one point of the island, and this brought him in view of a second; and there he remembered the wizard trees to have been growing by the score together in a wood. From this point there went up a hubbub of men crying not to be described; and by the sound of them, those that he ran with shaped their course for the same quarter. A little nearer, and there began to mingle with the outcry, the crash of many axes. And at this a thought came at last into his mind that the high chief had consented; that the men of the tribe had set to cutting down these trees; that word had gone about the isle from sorcerer to sorcerer, and these were all now assembling to defend their trees. Desire of strange things swept him on. He posted with the voices, crossed the beach, and came into the borders of the wood, and stood astonished. One tree had fallen, others were part hewed away. There was the tribe clustered. They were back to back, and bodies lay, and blood flowed among their feet. The hue of fear was on all their faces; their voices went up to heaven, shrill as a weasel's cry.

Have you seen a child when he is all alone and has a wooden sword, and fights, leaping and hewing with the empty air? Even so the man-eaters huddled back to back and heaved up their axes and laid on, and screamed as they laid on, and behold! no man to contend with them! Only here and there Keola saw an axe swinging over against them without hands; and time and again a man of the tribe would fall before it, clove in twain or burst asunder, and his soul sped howling.

For a while Keola looked upon this prodigy like one that dreams, and then fear took him by the midst as sharp as death, that he should behold such doings. Even in that same flash the high chief of the clan spied him standing, and pointed and called out his name. Then the whole tribe saw him also, and their eyes flashed, and their teeth clashed.

'I am too long here,' thought Keola, and ran farther out of the wood and down the beach, not caring whither.

'Keola!' said a voice close by upon the empty sand.

'Lehua! Is that you?' he cried, and gasped, and looked in vain for her; but by eyesight he was stark alone.

'I saw you pass before,' the voice answered; 'but you would not hear me. Quick! Get the leaves and the herbs, and let us flee.'

'You are there with the mat?' he asked.

'Here, at your side,' said she. And he felt her arms about him. 'Quick! The leaves and the herbs, before my father can get back!'

So Keola ran for his life, and fetched the wizard fuel; and Lehua guided him back, and set his feet upon the mat, and made the fire. All the time of its burning, the sound of the battle towered out of the wood; the wizards and the man-eaters hard at fight; the wizards, the viewless ones, roaring out aloud like bulls upon a mountain, and the men of the tribe replying shrill and savage out of the terror of their souls. And all the time of the burning, Keola stood there and listened, and shook, and watched how the unseen hands of Lehua poured the leaves. She poured them fast, and the flame burned high, and scorched Keola's hands; and she speeded and blew the burning with her breath. The last leaf was eaten, the flame fell, and the shock followed, and there were Keola and Lehua in the room at home.

Now, when Keola could see his wife at last he was mighty pleased, and he was mighty pleased to be home again in Molokai and sit down beside a bowl of *poi*—for they made no *poi* on board ships, and there was none in the Isle of Voices—and he was out of the body with pleasure to be clean escaped out of the hands of the eaters of men. But there was another matter not so clear, and Lehua and Keola talked of it all night and were troubled. There was Kalamake left upon the isle. If, by the blessing of God, he could but stick there, all were well; but should he escape and return to Molokai, it would be an ill day for his daughter and her husband They spoke of his gift of swelling and whether he could wade that distance in the seas. But Keola knew by this time where that island was—and that is to say, in the Low or Dangerous Archipelago. So they fetched the atlas and looked upon the distance in the map, and by what they could make of it, it seemed a far way for an old gentleman to walk. Still, it would not do to make too sure of a warlock like Kalamake, and they determined at last to take counsel of a white missionary.

So the first one that came by, Keola told him everything. And the missionary was very sharp on him for taking the second wife in the low island; but for all the rest, he vowed he could make neither head nor tail of it.

'However,' says he, 'if you think this money of your father is ill-gotten, my advice to you would be to give some of it to the lepers and some to the missionary fund. And as for this extraordinary rigmarole, you cannot do better than keep it to yourselves.'

But he warned the police at Honolulu that, by all he could make out, Kalamake and Keola had been coining false money, and it would not be amiss to watch them.

Keola and Lehua took his advice, and gave many dollars to the lepers. And no doubt the advice must have been good, for from that day to this, Kalamake has never more been heard of. But whether he was slain in the battle by the trees, or whether he is still kicking his heels upon the Isle of Voices, who shall say?

Some Early Australian Ghosts

Anonymous

In the spring of 1850, I was employed in driving a large herd of cattle from New England down into the Melbourne country. The grass was plentiful, and the cattle travelled along at their leisure across the wide plains which lie between the Lachlan, Murrumbidgee and Edward Rivers.

It was nearly sunset on a fine evening in August when we came to the crossing-place of the Edward; and driving the cattle down into an angle of the river, we camped close to the foot of the sandhill on which the township is built. There was a pretty large crowd around our campfire, and there was a long argument as to the best track across the Old Man Plain. Most of us were in favour of Lang's Crossing, but a stockman named Driscoll objected, asking, 'And how do you propose to avoid the Black Swamp and the ghost of the Trotting Cob?'

His objection was received with a roar of laughter; but Driscoll jumped up in a rage and said: 'You may laugh as much as you like, boys, but as sure as I am standing here, I saw it myself, worse luck, and seeing's believing!'

Of course, when we heard this, we were all anxious to hear the story. And Driscoll was soon prevailed upon to tell us his adventure.

'You all know Wantabadgery Station above Wagga-Wagga. Well, two years ago, Bill Kelly and I took three hundred fat beasts from there to Bendigo. The feed was good, and we came down the riverbank until we reached Lang's Crossing, where we took the cattle across. It was late in the afternoon when we got out on the plain, and the sun was just dipping as we were abreast of the Black Swamp; so we rounded up the cattle and decided to stop there for the night. We hobbled our horses close at hand, lit our fire and had our suppers. Then we agreed that I should take the first watch. Kelly rolled himself up in his possum rug, and I went down to have a look at the cattle and horses. I found them all right; so I went back to the fire, heaped on fresh fuel, and stretched myself out to have a comfortable smoke. I was pretty tired with riding all day, and the fire was hot, so in a short time I dozed off.

'I must have slept three or four hours, for the cold awoke me. I got up to put more wood on the fire, and then I thought I would just go round to check the cattle before I woke Kelly to take his watch. So I caught and saddled a mare, and rode off to the cattle range. The moon was at the full, and shining brightly, and the beasts had drawn out on the plain to feed. So I started to head them back. I was cantering along when all of a sudden the leading cattle came galloping back. As they wheeled, a man passed close to me, riding a bald-faced cob, and coming from the opposite direction. Now, Kelly's horse was bald-faced, and I thought he had woken up and come to look for me, so I rode on towards our camp. When I got there, I found Kelly lying quite snug, rolled up in his rug, fast asleep! Naturally I was quite put out.

'I shook him quite roughly, and when he sat up, I said: "Kelly, what do you mean by coming back and lying down again, when you know it's your watch?"

'"Lying down again?" he replied. "Why, I never got up until this moment."

'"What!" I cried. "Do you want to deny that you passed me just now on the plain, heading back the cattle? I did not see your face, but I saw the bald face of your horse plain enough."

'At that Kelly jumped up as though he'd been shot. "Saddle up for your life, Driscoll," said he, "and let us be off. You've seen the ghost of the Trotting Cob, and we're both dead men!"

'Well, we jumped on our horses and moved camp. And by daybreak we had camped just where we are now. But that very trip, Kelly was drowned in the Campaspe, and I broke two ribs and my collarbone, So I, for one, would sooner go a hundred miles round than camp again near the Black Swamp than chance seeing the ghost of the Trotting Cob.'

Incident At Myrtle Creek

There were still several who laughed at the idea of such things as ghosts. At last a bullock driver from the Sydney side said: 'There are ghosts, there's no denying. And I'll tell you of one that hundreds heard about and many of you know the man who saw it... Most of you have been up the Murray and have passed Brown's Station just above Quart. Well, when I was a government man doing my time, I was living near Brown's farm. He had just settled down at the Murray with a few hundred heads of cattle, and stopped there five or six months, putting up huts and yards and breaking in the cattle to the run. So when he thought everything was going well, he started for down-country, intending to bring up more stock. He travelled on horseback, for there were no mail-coaches then, and as he pushed on pretty sharp, he was very tired when he got to Myrtle Creek.

'Putting up at the Myrtle Creek inn, he told Thomson, the landlord, to call him early in the morning. He took his supper, and two or three glasses of rum, and went to bed. Towards morning something awoke him, and when he opened his eyes he saw his wife standing by the bedside. Before he could speak to her, she went out of the room. Well, Brown was greatly surprised at seeing her, but he got up and dressed, thinking she had come part of the way to meet him. When he went down, he looked into the parlour. And when he could not find her anywhere, he began calling out her name. The noise roused the landlord, who came and asked him what was going on.

'"Why," says Brown, "I want my wife. She's come and got me up, and now she's hidden herself."

'"You're dreaming, man," said the landlord. "How can your wife be here? You know she's at your Cow-pasture Farm."

'With that, Brown grew quite frightened. "Saddle my horse at once," said he, "for as sure as I'm a living man, my wife came and spoke to me tonight, and I'm greatly afraid that something has happened to her at home." And he mounted his horse and galloped off.

'He rode until he knocked up his horse, and then he borrowed a fresh one, and kept on as fast as he could ride, so that, before sunset, he came close to the Cow-pasture Farm. As he galloped up, he could see that something unusual was going on. Several horses were fastened to the posts of the verandah, the working men were standing in groups at the doors of their huts, and two or three troupers were lounging about near the stockyard. Brown jumped off his horse and was about to enter his house when one of his neighbours met him at the door. The neighbour led him away a little distance, and told him as gently as he could what had taken place. Now boys, Brown was a good master to his assigned servants, but his wife was a tyrant. And while he was at the Murray, she had been stopping the rations of the government men. There was one man in particular she took a dislike to; he could do nothing right, and almost every Monday morning she saw to it that he got fifty lashes at the nearest courthouse. At last he got desperate. He was chopping some wood, when she came up to him, and after abusing him, said: "I'll get you fifty more on Monday next." "I may get the fifty," said he, "but you'll not live to know of it." And with that he lifted the axe he had in his hand, and split her skull.

'This happened at the Cow-pastures at the very hour when she was seen by Brown in the inn at Myrtle Creek. So, you see, boys, there can be no doubt but ghosts do sometimes appear to us!'

The Cooee Hut

'Have you heard the story about the Cooee Hut?' asked Jim Darling, stirring up the fire. 'It's out at the Yareko Creek, and the way it got its name was this: at the time the Billilong and Yareko were first settled on, there was a man named Bill White employed at the Goree Station. He was an emigrant, and had not been long in the colony, so they used to keep him about the place chopping wood and carting water. Well, it so happened that one of the shepherds had a row with the overseer and got discharged at once; so, as they had no one else handy, they decided to send Bill White shepherding until they could get another man. The hut is twenty-five miles back from Goree; so the overseer went out himself with Bill and the sheep, and then stopped a day with him, to show him the run. Bill had no hut-keeper, but he managed pretty well for two or three days.

'One very hot day he must have fallen asleep in the middle of the day, when the sheep were in camp, and did not awake until they were drawn out. He was, as I told you, a new churn, and did not know anything about tracking, so he wandered vaguely up and down, looking for the flock, until he lost himself completely. Dusk was coming on, so he began cooeeing until he was fairly worn out, and then lay down to sleep. Next morning he started again, but he had got confused by then. You know the Yareko country is very puzzling, for the sandhills and plains are so much alike, it's very hard to tell one from another. Well, poor Bill tried to travel by the sun; but as he kept following it, he went round and round, and at dusk was near the place he started from. He had no food, and could not find the creek, so he was dying of thirst, for it was burning hot weather. He cooeed again and again, until he fell exhausted. And there he lay until morning.

'In the morning he got up and crawled a few yards. Then down he sank, and there he perished.

'Meanwhile, the sheep had gone to another outstation, ten miles further back, where they had been running formerly. As the feed was good, they stopped there very contentedly for seven or eight days. The overseer happened to see them, and of course he brought them into the home station, and then went out to tell Bill White to come in himself.

'When the overseer got to the hut, he found the ashes cold on the hearth; and he could see that White had not been in for some days. In a great fright he galloped back to the home station, where he mustered all hands to go and look for Bill. He took two aboriginal trackers along. And as I happened to be passing, I joined them.

'Well, it was near dusk when we got to the hut, and of course we could do nothing that night, so we hobbled the horses and went into the hut. We were just getting our suppers when we heard a faint cooee, and then another and another. We answered at once, for we were hoping that it was Bill White coming up; but the sound came no nearer, though the cooee was repeated every four or five minutes. We thought that perhaps he had been hurt and could not walk, so several of us went out to look for him. But we could see nothing of Bill, though the cooeeing continued and apparently quite close to us. After about an hour, it ceased suddenly. We went back to the hut, greatly puzzled and very uneasy.

'Next morning at daylight we started out, and the trackers very soon found poor Bill's trail. It was through them that I am able to tell you of his rambling about, for they traced all his wanderings, pointed out where he sat and where he slept, and at last brought us to where his body lay. And strange to relate, he had died within less than a mile of his home.

'We buried him in an adjacent sandhill, where you may see his grave fenced in. But since that time, no one will live in that hut, for every evening, from dusk until dark, poor Bill White is heard cooeeing. Many who had never heard this story, and chanced to camp in the neighbourhood, have heard the cooeeing and have imagined that some traveller was approaching, little realizing that it was the spirit of Bill White wandering about the Cooee Hut.'

(Retold by Ruskin Bond from an article in
Chambers's Journal for July–December 1863)

Thurnley Abbey

Perceval Landon

Three years ago I was on my way out to the East, and as an extra day in London was of some importance, I took the Friday evening mail-train to Brindisi instead of the usual Thursday morning Marseilles Express. Many people shrink from the long forty-eight hour train journey through Europe, and the subsequent rush across the Mediterranean on the nineteen-knot *Isis* or *Osiris;* but there is really very little discomfort on either the train or the mail-boat, and unless there is actually nothing for one to do, I always like to save the extra day and a half in London before I say goodbye to her for one of my longer tramps. This time—it was early, I remember, in the shipping season, probably about the beginning of September—there were few passengers, and I had a compartment in the P&O Indian Express to myself all the way from Calais. All Sunday I watched the blue waves dimpling the Adriatic, and the pale rosemary along the cuttings; the plain white towns, with their flat roofs and their bold 'duomos', and the grey-green gnarled olive orchards of Apulia. The journey was just like any other.

We ate in the dining car as often and as long as we decently could. We slept after luncheon; we dawdled the afternoon away with yellow-backed novels; sometimes we exchanged platitudes in the smoking room, and it was there that I met Alastair Colvin.

Colvin was a man of middle height, with a resolute, well-cut jaw; his hair was turning grey; his moustache was sun-whitened, otherwise he was clean-shaven—obviously a gentleman, and obviously also a preoccupied man. He had no great wit. When spoken to, he made the usual remarks in the right way, and I dare say he refrained from banalities only because he spoke less than the rest of us; most of the time he buried himself in the Wagon-lit Company's timetable, but seemed unable to concentrate his attention on any one page of it. He found that I had been over the Siberian railway, and for a quarter of an hour he discussed it with me. Then he lost interest in it, and rose to go to his compartment. But he came back again very soon, and seemed glad to pick up the conversation again.

Of course, this did not seem to me to be of any importance. Most travellers by train become a trifle infirm of purpose after thirty-six hours' rattling. But Colvin's restless way I noticed in somewhat marked contrast with the man's personal importance and dignity; especially ill-suited was it to his finely made large hand with strong, broad, regular nails and its few lines. As I looked at his hand I noticed a long, deep, and recent scar of ragged shape. However, it is absurd to pretend that I thought anything was unusual. I went off at five o'clock on Sunday afternoon to sleep away the hour or two that had still to be got through before we arrived at Brindisi.

Once there, we few passengers transhipped our hand baggage, verified our berths—there were only a score of us in all—and then, after an aimless ramble of half an hour in

Brindisi, we returned to dinner at the Hotel International, not wholly surprised that the town had been the death of Virgil. If I remember rightly, there is a gaily painted hall at the International—I do not wish to advertise anything, but there is no other place in Brindisi at which to await the coming of the mails—and after dinner I was looking with awe at a trellis overgrown with blue vines, when Colvin moved across the room to my table. He picked up *Il Secolo,* but almost immediately gave up the pretence of reading it. He turned squarely to me and said:

'Would you do me a favour?'

One doesn't do favours to stray acquaintances on Continental Expresses without knowing something more of them than I knew of Colvin. But I smiled in a non-committal way, and asked him what he wanted. I wasn't wrong in part of my estimate of him; he said bluntly:

'Will you let me sleep in your cabin on the *Osiris?*' And he coloured a little as he said it.

Now, there is nothing more tiresome than having to put up with a stable-companion at sea, and I asked him rather pointedly: 'Surely, there is room for all of us?' I thought that perhaps he had been partnered off with some mangy Levantine, and wanted to escape from him at all hazards.

Colvin, still somewhat confused, said: 'Yes; I am in a cabin by myself. But you would do me the greatest favour if you would allow me to share yours.'

This was all very well, but, besides the fact that I always sleep better when alone, there had been some recent thefts on board English liners, and I hesitated, frank and honest and self-conscious as Colvin was. Just then the mail-train came in with a clatter and a rush of escaping steam, and I asked him to see me again about it on the boat when we started. He answered me curtly—I suppose he saw the mistrust in my manner—'I am a member of White's.' I smiled to myself as he said it, but I remembered in a moment that the man—if he were really what he claimed to be, and I make no doubt that he was—must have been sorely put to it before he urged the fact as a guarantee of his respectability to a total stranger at a Brindisi hotel.

That evening, as we cleared the red and green harbour—lights of Brindisi, Colvin explained. This is his story in his own words.

'When I was travelling in India some years ago, I made the acquaintance of a youngish man in the Forests Service. We camped out together for a week, and I found him a pleasant companion. John Broughton was a light-hearted soul when off duty, but a steady and capable man in any of the small emergencies that continually arise in that department. He was liked and trusted by Indians and though a trifle over-pleased with himself when he escaped to civilization at Simla or Calcutta, Broughton's future was well-assured in Government service, when a fair-sized estate was unexpectedly left to him, and he joyfully shook the dust to the Indian plains from his feet and returned to England. For five years he drifted about London. I saw him now and then. We dined together about every eighteen months, and I could trace pretty exactly the gradual sickening of Broughton with a merely idle life. He then set out on a couple of long voyages, returned as restless as before, and at last told me that he had decided to marry and settle down at his place, Thurnley Abbey, which had long been empty. He spoke about looking after the property and standing for his constituency in the usual way. Vivien Wilde, his fiancée, had, I suppose, begun to take him in hand. She was a pretty girl with a deal of fair hair and rather an exclusive manner; deeply religious in a narrow school, she was still kindly and high-spirited, and I thought that Broughton was in luck. He was quite happy and full of information about his future.

'Among other things, I asked him about Thurnley Abbey. He confessed that he hardly knew the place. The last tenant, a man called Clarke, had lived in one wing for fifteen years and seen no one. He had been a miser and a hermit. It was the rarest thing for a light to be seen at the Abbey after dark. Only the barest necessities of life were ordered, and the tenant himself received them at the side door. His one half caste manservant, after a month's stay in the house, had abruptly left without warning, and had returned to the Southern States. One thing Broughton complained bitterly about: Clarke had wilfully spread the rumour among the villagers that the Abbey was haunted, and had even condescended to play childish tricks with spirit lamps and salt in order to scare trespassers away at night. He had been detected in the act of this tomfoolery, but the story spread, and no one, said Broughton, would venture near the house except in broad daylight. The hauntedness of Thurnley Abbey was now, he said with a grin, part of the gospel of the countryside, but he and his young wife were going to change all that. Would I propose myself any time I liked? I, of course, said I would, and equally, of course, intended to I do nothing of the sort without a definite invitation.

'The house was put in thorough repair, though not a stick of the old furniture and tapestry were removed. Floors and ceilings were relaid: the roof was made watertight again, and the dust of half a century was scoured out. He showed me some photographs of the place. It was called an Abbey, though as a matter of fact it had been only the infirmary of the long vanished Abbey of Closter some five miles away. The larger part of this building remained as it had been in pre-Reformation days, but a wing had been added in Jacobean times, and that part of the house had been kept in something like repair by Mr Clarke. He had in both the ground and first floors set a heavy timber door, strongly barred with iron, in the passage between the earlier and the Jacobean parts of the house, and had entirely neglected the former. So there had been a good deal of work to be done.

'Broughton, whom I saw in London two or three times about this period, made a deal of fun over the positive refusal of the workmen to remain after sundown. Even after the electric light had been put into every room, nothing would induce them to remain, though, as Broughton observed, electric light was death on ghosts. The legend of the Abbey's ghosts had gone far and wide, and the men would take no risks. They went home in batches of five and six, and even during the daylight hours there was an inordinate amount of talking between one and another, if either happened to be out of sight of his companion. On the whole, though nothing of any sort or kind had been conjured tip even by their heated imaginations during their five months' work upon the Abbey, the belief in the ghosts was rather strengthened than otherwise in Thurnley because of the men's confessed nervousness, and local tradition declared itself in favour of the ghost of an immured nun.'

'"Good old nun!" said Broughton.

'I asked him whether in general he believed in the possibility of ghosts, and, rather to my surprise, he said that he couldn't say he entirely disbelieved in them. A man in India had told him one morning in camp that he believed that his mother was dead in England, as her vision had come to his tent the night before. He had not been alarmed, but had said nothing, and the figure vanished again. As a matter of fact, the next possible dak-walla brought on a telegram announcing the mother's death. "There the thing was," said Broughton. But at Thurnley he was practical enough. He roundly cursed the idiotic selfishness of Clarke, whose silly antics had caused all the inconvenience. At the same time, he couldn't refuse to sympathize to some extent with the ignorant workmen. 'My own idea,' said he, 'is that if a ghost ever does come in one's way, one ought to speak to it.'

'I agreed. Little as I knew of the ghost world and its conventions, I had always remembered that a spook was in honour bound to wait to be spoken to. It didn't seem much to do, and I felt that the sound of one's own voice would at any rate reassure oneself as to one's wakefulness. But there are few ghosts outside Europe—few, that is, that a white man can see—and I had never been troubled with any. However, as I have said, I told Broughton that I agreed.

'So the wedding took place, and I went to it in a tall hat which I bought for the occasion, and the new Mrs Broughton smiled very nicely at me afterwards. As it had to happen, I took the Orient Express that evening and was not in England again for nearly six months. Just before I came back I got a letter from Broughton. He asked if I could see him in London or come to Thurnley, as he thought I should be better able to help him than anyone else he knew. His wife sent a nice message to me at the end, so I was reassured about at least one thing. I wrote from Budapest that I would come and see him at Thurnley two days after my arrival in London, and as I sauntered out of the Pannonia into the Kerepesi Utcza to post my letters, I wondered of what earthly service I could be to Broughton. I had been out with him after tiger on foot, and I could imagine few men better able at a pinch to manage their own business. However, I had nothing to do, so after dealing with some small accumulations of business during my absence, I packed a kit-bag and departed to Euston.

'I was met by Broughton's great limousine at Thurnley Road station, and after a drive of nearly seven miles we echoed through the sleepy streets of Thurnley village, into which the main gates of the park thrust themselves, splendid with pillars and spread eagles and tomcats rampant atop of them. I never was a herald, but I know that the Broughtons have the right to supporters—Heaven knows why! From the gates a quadruple avenue of beech trees led inwards for a quarter of a mile. Beneath them a neat strip of fine turf edged the road and ran back until the poison of the dead beech leaves killed it under the trees. There were many wheel tracks on the road, and a comfortable little pony trap jogged past me laden with a country parson and his wife and daughter. Evidently there was some garden party going on at the Abbey. The road dropped away to the right at the end of the avenue, and I could see the Abbey across a wide pasturage and a broad lawn thickly dotted with guests.

'The end of the building was plain. It must have been almost mercilessly austere when it was first built, but time had crumbled the edges and toned the stone down to an orange-lichened grey wherever it showed behind its curtain of magnolia, jasmine, and ivy. Farther on was the three-storeyed Jacobean house, tall and handsome. There had not been the slightest attempt to adapt the one to the other, but the kindly ivy had glossed over the touching point. There was a tall fleche in the middle of the building, surmounting a small, bell tower. Behind the house there rose the mountainous verdure of Spanish chestnuts all the way up the hill.

'Broughton had seen me coming from afar, and walked

across from his other guests to welcome me before turning me over to the butler's care. This man was sandy-haired and rather inclined to be talkative. He could, however, answer hardly any questions about the house; he had, he said, only been there three weeks. Mindful of what Broughton had told me, I made no inquiries about ghosts, though the room into which I was shown might have justified anything. It was a very large low room with oak beams projecting from the white ceiling. Every inch of the walls, including the doors, was covered with tapestry, and a remarkably fine Italian four post bedstead, heavily draped, added to the darkness and dignity of the place. All the furniture was old, well-made, and dark. Underfoot there was a plain green pile carpet, the only new thing about the room except the electric light fittings and the jugs and basins. Even the looking glass on the dressing table was an old pyramidal Venetian glass set in heavy repousse frame of tarnished silver.

'After a few minutes' cleaning up, I went downstairs and out upon the lawn, where I greeted my hostess. The people gathered there were of the usual country type, all anxious to be pleased and roundly curious as to the new master of the Abbey. Rather to my surprise, and quite to my pleasure, I rediscovered Glenham, whom I had known well in old days in Barotseland; he lived quite close, as, he remarked with a grin, I ought to have known. "But," he added, "I don't live in a place like this." He swept his hand to the long, low lines of the Abbey in obvious admiration, and then, to my intense interest, muttered beneath his breath, "Thank God!" He saw that I had overheard him, and turning to me said decidedly, "Yes, 'thank God' I said, and I meant it. I wouldn't live at the Abbey for all Broughton's money."

"But surely," I demurred, "you know that old Clarke was discovered in the very act of setting light to his bug-a-boos?"

'Glenham shrugged his shoulders. "Yes, I know about that. But there is something wrong with the place still. All I can say is that Broughton is a different man since he has lived here. I don't believe that he will remain much longer. But—you're staying here? Well, you'll hear all about it tonight. There's a big dinner, I understand." The conversation turned off to old reminiscences, and Glenham soon after had to go.

'Before I went to dress that evening I had twenty minutes' talk with Broughton in his library. There was no doubt that the man was altered, gravely altered. He was nervous and fidgety, and I found him looking at me only when my eye was off him. I naturally asked him what he wanted of me. I told him I would do anything I could, but that I couldn't conceive what he lacked that I could provide. He said with a lustreless smile that there was, however, something, and that he would tell me the following morning. It struck me that he was somehow ashamed of himself. And perhaps ashamed of the part he was asking me to play. However, I dismissed the subject from my mind and went up to dress in my palatial room. As I shut the door a draught blew out the Queen of Sheba from the wall, and I noticed that the tapestries were not fastened to the wall at the bottom. I have always held very practical views about spooks, and it has often seemed to me that the slow waving in firelight of loose tapestry upon a wall would account for ninety-nine per cent of the stories one hears. Certainly, the dignified undulation of this lady with her attendants and huntsmen—one of whom was untidily cutting the throat of a fallow deer upon the very steps on which King Solomon, a grey-faced Flemish nobleman with the order of the Golden Fleece, awaited his fair visitor—gave colour to my hypothesis.

'Nothing much happened at dinner. The people were very

much like those of the garden party. A young woman next me seemed anxious to know what was being read in London. As she was far more familiar than I with the most recent magazines and literary supplements, I found salvation in being myself instructed in the tendencies of modern fiction. All true art, she said, was shot through and through with melancholy. How vulgar were the attempts at wit that marked so many modern books! From the beginning of literature it had always been tragedy that embodied the highest attainment of every age. To call such works morbid merely begged the question. No thoughtful man—she looked sternly at me through the steel rim of her glasses—could fail to agree with me. Of course, as one would, I immediately and properly said that I slept with Pett Ridge and Jacobs under my pillow at night, and that if *Jorrocks* weren't quite so large and cornery, I would add him to the company. She hadn't read any of them, so I was saved—for a time. But I remember grimly that she said that the clearest wish of her life was to be in some awful and soul-freezing situation of horror, and I remember that she dealt hardly with the hero of Nat Paynter's vampire story, between nibbles at her brown bread ice. She was a cheerless soul, and I couldn't help thinking that if there were many such in the neighbourhood, it was not surprising that old Glenham had been stuffed with some nonsense or the other about the Abbey. Yet, nothing could well have been less creepy than the glitter of silver and glass, and the subdued lights and cackle of conversation all round the dinner table.

'After the ladies had gone I found myself talking to the rural dean. He was a thin, earnest man, who at once turned the conversation to old Clarke's buffooneries. But, he said, Mr Broughton had introduced such a new and cheerful spirit, not only into the Abbey, but, he might say, into the whole neighbourhood, that he had great hopes that the ignorant superstitions of the past were from henceforth destined to oblivion. Thereupon his other neighbour, a portly gentleman of independent means and position, audibly remarked "Amen", which damped the rural dean, and we talked of partridges past, partridges present, and pheasants to come. At the other end of the table Broughton sat with a couple of his friends, red-faced hunting men. Once I noticed that they were discussing me, but I paid no attention to it at the time. I remembered it a few hours later.

'By eleven all the guests were gone, and Broughton, his wife, and I were alone together under the fine plaster ceiling of the Jacobean drawing room. Mrs Broughton talked about one or two of the neighbours, and then, with a smile, said that she knew I would excuse her, shook hands with me, and went off to bed. I am not very good at analysing things, but I felt that she talked a little uncomfortably and with a suspicion of effort, smiled rather conventionally, and was obviously glad to go. These things seem trifling enough to repeat, but I had throughout the faint feeling that everything was not square. Under the circumstances, this was enough to set me wondering what on earth the service could be that I was to render—wondering also whether the whole business were not some ill-advised jest in order to make me come down from London for a mere shooting-party.

'Broughton said little after she had gone. But he was evidently labouring to bring the conversation round to the so-called haunting of the Abbey. As soon as I saw this, of course I asked him directly about it. He then seemed at once to lose interest in the matter. There was no doubt about it; Broughton was somehow a changed man, and to my mind he had changed in no way for the better. Mrs Broughton seemed no sufficient cause. He was clearly very fond of her, and she of him. I reminded him that he was going to tell me what I could do for him in the morning, pleaded my journey, lighted a candle, and went upstairs with him. At the end of the passage leading into the old house he grinned weakly and said, "Mind, if you see a ghost, do talk to it; you said you would." He stood irresolutely a moment and then turned away. At the door of his dressing room he paused once more: "I'm here," he called out, "if you should want anything. Good night," and he shut his door.

'I went along the passage to my room, undressed, switched on a lamp beside my bed, read a few pages of *The Jungle Book*, and then, more than ready for sleep, turned the light off and went fast asleep.

'Three hours later I woke up. There was not a breath of wind outside. There was not even a flicker of light from the fireplace. As I lay there, an ash tinkled slightly as it cooled, but there was hardly a gleam of the dullest red in the grate. An owl cried among the silent Spanish chestnuts on the slope outside. I idly reviewed the events of the day, hoping that I should fall off to sleep again before I reached dinner. But at the end I seemed as wakeful as ever. There was no help for it. I must read my *Jungle Book* again till I felt ready to go off, so I fumbled for the pear at the end of the cord that hung down inside the bed, and I switched on the bedside lamp. The sudden glory dazzled me for a moment. I felt under my pillow for my book with half-shut eyes. Then, growing used to the light, I happened to look down to the foot of my bed.

'I can never tell you really what happened then. Nothing I could ever confess in the most abject words could even faintly picture to you what I felt. I know that my heart stopped dead, and my throat shut automatically. In one instinctive movement I crouched back up against the headboards of the bed, staring at the horror. The movement set my heart going again, and the sweat dripped from every pore. I am not a particularly religious man, but I had always believed that God would never allow any supernatural appearance to present itself to man in such a guise and in such circumstances that harm, either bodily or mental, could result to him. I can only tell you that at that moment both my life and my reason rocked unsteadily on their seats.'

The other *Osiris* passengers had gone to bed. Only he and I remained leaning over the starboard railing, which rattled uneasily now and then under the fierce vibration of the over-engined mail-boat. Far over, there were the lights of a few fishing-smacks riding out the night, and a great rush of white combing and seething water fell out and away from us overside.

At last Colvin went on:

'Leaning over the foot of my bed, looking at me, was a figure swathed in a rotten and tattered veiling. This shroud passed over the head, but left both eyes and the right side of the face bare. It then followed the line of the arm down to where the hand grasped the bed-end. The face was not entirely that of a skull, though the eyes and the flesh of the face were totally gone. There was a thin, dry skin drawn tightly over the features, and there was some skin left on the hand. One wisp of hair crossed the forehead. It was perfectly still. I looked at it, and it looked at me, and my brains turned dry and hot in my head. I had still got the pear of the electric lamp in my hand, and I played idly with it; only I dared not turn the light out again. I shut my eyes, only to open them in a hideous terror the same second. The thing had not moved. My heart was thumping, and the sweat cooled me as it evaporated. Another cinder tinkled in the grate, and a panel creaked in the wall.

'My reason failed me. For twenty minutes, or twenty seconds, I was able to think of nothing else but this awful figure, till there came, hurtling through the empty channels of my senses, the remembrance that Broughton and his friends had discussed me furtively at dinner. The dim possibility of its being a hoax stole gratefully into my unhappy mind, and once there, one's pluck came creeping back along a thousand tiny veins. My first sensation was one of blind unreasoning thankfulness that my brain was going to stand the trial. I am not a timid man, but the best of us needs some human handle to steady him in time to extremity, and in this faint but growing hope that after all it might be only a brutal hoax, I found the fulcrum that I needed. At last I moved.

'How I managed to do it I cannot tell you, but with one spring towards the foot of the bed I got within arm's length and struck out one fearful blow with my fist at the thing. It crumbled under it, and my hand was cut to the bone. With a sickening revulsion after my terror, I dropped half-fainting across the end of the bed. So it was merely a foul trick after all. No doubt the trick had been played many a time before; no doubt Broughton and his friends had had some large bet among themselves as to what I should do when I discovered the gruesome thing. From my state of abject terror I found myself transported into an insensate anger. I shouted curses upon Broughton. I dived rather than climbed over the bed-end on to the sofa. I tore at the robed skeleton—how well the whole thing had been carried out, I thought—I broke the skull against the floor, and stamped upon its dry bones. I flung the head away under the bed, and rent the brittle bones of the trunk in pieces. I snapped the thin thigh bones across my knee, and flung them in different directions. The shin bones I set up against a stool and broke with my heel. I raged like a Berserker against the loathly thing, and stripped the ribs from the backbone and slung the breastbone against the cupboard. My fury increased as the work of destruction went on. I tore the frail rotten veil into twenty pieces, and the dust went up over everything, over the clean blotting paper and the silver inkstand. At last my work was done. There was but a raffle of broken bones and strips of parchment and crumbling wool. Then, picking up a piece of the skull—it was the check and temple bone of the right side, I remember—I opened the door and went down the passage to Broughton's dressing room. I remember still how my sweat dripping pyjamas clung to me as I walked. At the door I kicked and entered.

'Broughton was in bed. He had already turned the light on and seemed shrunken and horrified. For a moment he could hardly pull himself together. Then I spoke. I don't know what I said. Only I know that from a heart full and overfull with hatred and contempt, spurred on by shame of my own recent cowardice, I let my tongue run on. He answered nothing. I was amazed at my own fluency. My hair still clung lankily to my wet temples, my hand was bleeding profusely, and I must have looked a strange sight. Broughton huddled himself up at the head of the bed just as I had. Still he made no answer, no answer, no defence. He seemed preoccupied with something besides my reproaches, and once or twice moistened his lips with his tongue. But he could say nothing though he moved his hands now and then, just as a baby who cannot speak moves its hands.

'At last the door into Mrs Broughton's room opened and she came in, white and terrified. "What is it? What is it? Oh, in God's name! What is it?" she cried again and again, and then she went up to her husband and sat on the bed in her nightdress, and the two faced me. I told her what the matter was. I spared her husband not a word for her presence there. Yet, he seemed hardly to understand. I told the pair that I had spoiled their cowardly joke for them. Broughton looked up.

"'I have smashed the foul thing into a hundred pieces," I said. Broughton licked his lips again and his mouth worked. "By God!" I shouted, "It would serve you right if I thrashed you within an inch of your life. I will take care that not a decent man or woman of my acquaintance ever speaks to you again." "And there," I added, throwing the broken piece of the skull upon the floor beside his bed, "there is a souvenir for you, of your damned work tonight!"

'Broughton saw the bone, and in a moment it was his turn to frighten me. He squealed like a hare caught in a trap. He screamed and screamed till Mrs Broughton, almost as bewildered as myself, held on to him and coaxed him like a child to be quiet. But Broughton—and as he moved I thought that ten minutes ago I perhaps looked as terribly ill as he did—thrust her from him, and scrambled out of the bed on to the floor, and still screaming put out his hand to the bone. It had blood on it from my hand. He paid no attention to me whatever. In truth I said nothing. This was a new turn indeed to the horrors of the evening. He rose from the floor with the bone in his hand and stood silent. He seemed to be listening. "Time, time, perhaps," he muttered, and almost at the same moment fell at full length on the carpet, cutting his head against the fender. The bone flew from his hand and came to rest near the door. I picked Broughton up, haggard and broken, with blood over face. He whispered hoarsely and quickly, "Listen, listen!" We listened.

'After ten seconds' utter quiet, I seemed to hear something. I could not be sure, but at last there was no doubt. There was a quiet sound as of one moving along the passage. Little regular steps came towards us over the hard oak flooring. Broughton moved to where his wife sat, white and speechless, on the bed, and pressed her face into his shoulder.

'Then, the last thing that I could see as he turned the light out, he fell forward with his own head pressed into the pillow of the bed. Something in their company, something in their cowardice, helped me, and I faced the open doorway of the room, which was outlined fairly clearly against the dimly lighted passage. I put out one hand and touched Mrs Broughton's shoulder in the darkness. But at the last moment I too failed. I sank on my knees and put my face in the bed. Only we all heard. The footsteps came to the door, and there they stopped. The piece of bone was lying a yard inside the door. There was a rustle of moving stuff, and the thing was in the room. Mrs Broughton was silent: I could hear Broughton's voice praying, muffled in the pillow; I was cursing my own cowardice. Then the steps moved out again on the oak boards of the passage, and I heard the sounds dying away. In a flash of remorse I went to the door and looked out. At the end of the corridor I thought I saw something that moved away. A moment later the passage was empty. I stood with my forehead against the jamb of the door almost physically sick.

'"You can turn the light on," I said, and there was an answering flare. There was no bone at my feet. Mrs Broughton had fainted. Broughton was almost useless, and it took me ten minutes to bring her to. Broughton only said one thing worth remembering. For the most part he went on muttering prayers. But I was glad afterwards to recollect that he had said that thing. He said in a colourless voice, half as a question, half as a reproach, "You didn't speak to her."

'We spent the remainder of the night together. Mrs Broughton actually fell off into a kind of sleep before dawn, but she suffered so horribly in her dreams that I shook her into consciousness again. Never was dawn so long in coming. Three or four times Broughton spoke to himself. Mrs Broughton would then just tighten her hold on his arm, but she could say nothing. As for me, I can honestly say that I grew worse as the hours passed and the light strengthened. The two violent reactions had battered down my steadiness of view, and I felt that the foundations of my life had been built upon the sand. I said nothing, and after binding up my hand with a towel, I did not move. It was better so. They helped me and I helped them, and we all three knew that our reason had gone very near to ruin that night. At last, when the light came in pretty strongly, and the birds outside were chattering and singing, we felt that we must do something. Yet we never moved. You might have thought that we should particularly dislike being found as we were by the servants; yet nothing of that kind mattered a straw, and an overpowering listlessness bound us as we sat, until Chapman, Broughton's man, actually knocked and opened the door. None of us moved. Broughton, speaking hardly and stiffly, said, "Chapman, you can come back in five minutes." Chapman, was a discreet man, but it would have made no difference to us if he had carried his news to the "room" at once.

'We looked at each other and I said I must go back. I meant to wait outside till Chapman returned. I simply dared not re-enter my bedroom alone. Broughton roused himself and said that he would come with me. Mrs Broughton agreed to remain in her own room for five minutes if the blinds were drawn up and all the doors left open.

'So Broughton and I, leaning stiffly one against the other, went down to my room. By the morning light that filtered past the blinds we could see our way, and I released the blinds. There was nothing wrong in the room from end to end, except smears of my own blood at the end of the bed, on the sofa, and on the carpet where I had torn the thing to pieces.'

Colvin had finished his story. There was nothing to say. Seven bells stuttered out from the fo'c'sle, and the answering cry wailed through the darkness. I took him downstairs.

'Of course, I am much better now, but it is a kindness of you to let me sleep in your cabin.'

The Frontier Guards

H. Russell Wakefield

What a charming little house!' said Brinton, as he was walking in from a round of golf at Ellesborough with Lander.

'Yes, from the outside,' replied Lander.

'What's the matter with the inside-Eozoic plumbing?'

'No; the "usual offices" are neat, if not gaudy. Spengler would probably describe them as "contemporary with the death of Lincoln," but it's not that—it's haunted.'

'Is it, by Jove?' said Brinton, gazing up at it. 'Fancy such a dear little Queen Anne piece having such a nasty reputation. I see it's unoccupied.'

'It usually is,' replied Lander. 'Tell me about it.'

'During dinner I will. But you seem to find something of interest about those windows on the second floor.' Brinton gazed up for a moment or two longer, and then started to walk back in silence beside his host.

In a few minutes they reached Lander's cottage—it was rather more pretentious than that—an engaging two-storeyed structure added to and modernized from time to time, formerly known as 'the Old Vicarage', and rechristened 'Laymer's'. Black and white and creeper-lined, with a trim little garden of rose trees and mellow turf, two fine limes, and a great yew, impenetrable and secret. This little garden melted into an arable expanse, and there was a lovely view over to some high Chiltern spurs. The whole place just suited Lander, who was—or it might be more accurate to say, wanted to be—a novelist; a commonplace and ill-advised ambition, but he had money of his own and could afford to wait.

James Brinton, his guest for a week and a very old friend, occupied himself with a picture gallery in Mayfair. A very small gallery—one rather small room, to be exact—but he had admirable taste and made it pay.

Two hours later they sat down to dinner. 'Now then,' said Brinton, as Mrs Dunkley brought in the soup, 'tell me about that house.'

'Well,' replied Lander, 'I have had, as you know, much more experience of such places than most people, and I consider Pailton the worst or the best specimen I have heard or read of or experienced. For one thing, it is a "killer". The majority of haunted houses are harmless, the peculiar energy they have absorbed and radiate forth is not hostile to life. But in others the radiation is malignant and fatal. Pailton has been rented five times in the last twelve years; in each case the tenancy has been marked by a violent death within its walls. For my part, I have no two opinions concerning the morality of letting it at all. It should be razed to the ground.'

'How long do its occupants stick it out as a rule?'

'Six weeks is the record, and that was made by some person called Pendexter. That was three years ago. I knew Pendexter pére, and he was a courageous and determined person. His daughter was hurled down the stairs one night and killed, and I shall never forget the mingled fury and grief with which he told me about it. Previous to that he had detected eighteen different examples of psychic action—appearances and sounds—several definitely malignant. The family had not enjoyed one single day of freedom from abnormal phenomena.'

'How long since it was last occupied?' asked Brinton.

'It has been empty for a year, and I am inclined to think it will remain so. Any one who comes down to look at it is given a pretty straight tip by one or other of us to keep away.'

'Does it affect you violently?'

'I have never set foot in it.'

'What? You, of all people!'

'My dear Jim, just for that very reason. When I first discovered I was psychic I felt flattered and anxious to experience all I could. I soon changed my mind. I found I experienced quite enough without any need for making opportunities. I do to this day. Several times I have had a visitor in the study here after dinner, an uninvited guest. And it has always been so. I have many times heard and seen things which could not be explained in places with perfectly clean bills of psychic health. And one never gets quite used to it. Terror may pass, but some distress of mind is invariable. Any person gifted or afflicted like myself will tell you the same. It seems to me sometimes as if I actually assist in evoking and materializing these appearances, that I help to establish a connection between them and the place I inhabit, that I am a most unpleasant kind of lightning conductor.'

'Is there any possible explanation for that?'

'Well, I have formed one, but it would take rather a long time to explain, and may be quite fallacious. Anyhow, there has never been any need for me to visit such places as Pailton, and

I keep away from them if I can.'

'Would you very much object to going in for a minute or two?'

'Why?'

'Well, I have been bothered all my life about this business of ghosts. I have never seen one; in a sense I "don't believe in them", yet I am convinced you have known many. It is a maddening dualism of mind. I feel if I could just once come in contact with something of the kind I should feel a sense of enormous relief.'

'And you'd like me to conduct you over Pailton?'

'Not if it would really upset you.'

'It would be at your own risk,' said Lander, smiling.

'I'll risk it!'

'You mustn't imagine that you can go into a disturbed spot such as this and expect to see about ten ghosts in as many minutes. Even in the case of such a busy hive as Pailton there are many quiet periods, and some people simply cannot see ghosts. The odds are very much against your desire being granted, though, if you *are* psychic, the atmosphere of the place would affect you at once.'

'How?'

'Well, you've often heard of people who know by some obscure but infallible instinct that there's a cat in the room. Just so. However, I'll certainly give you the chance. It won't seriously disturb me. I can get the key in the morning from the woman who looks after it, though I need hardly say she doesn't sleep there. There is no need for a caretaker. It was broken into once, but the burglar was found dead in the dining room and since then the crooks have given it a wide berth.'

'It really is dangerous, then?'

'Beginning to feel a bit prudent?'

'No, I shall feel safe with you.'

'Very well then. After coming back from golf we'll pay it a visit. It will be dark by five, and we'll make the excursion about six. The chances of gratifying your curiosity will be better after dark. I'd better tell you something else. I never quite know how these places are going to affect me. Before now, I have gone off into a kind of trance and been decidedly weird, my dear Jim. My sense of time and space becomes distorted, though for your assurance I may say,' he added smiling, 'I am never dangerous when in this condition. Furthermore, you must be prepared to make acquaintance with a mode of existence in which the ordinary laws of existence which you have always known abdicate themselves. Bierce called his famous book of ghost stories, *Can These Things Be?* Assuredly they can. Now I'm sounding pompous and pontifical, but some such warning is necessary. When I touch that front door tomorrow I may become, in a sense, a stranger to you; once inside we shall cross a frontier into a region with its own laws of time and space, and where the seemingly impossible can happen... Do you understand what I mean and still want to go?'

'Yes,' replied Brinton, 'to all your questions.'

'Very well then,' said Lander, 'I will now get out the chess men and discover a complete answer to Reti's opening which you sprang on me last night; so you shall have the white pieces.'

November 21st was a lazy, drowsy, cloudless day, starting with a sharp ground frost which, thawing unresistingly as the sun climbed, made the tees at Ellesborough like tiny slides. In consequence, neither Brinton nor Lander played very good golf. This upset Brinton not at all, for he was thinking much more of that which was beginning to impress him as a possible ordeal, the crossing of the threshold of Pailton a few hours later. As they finished their second round, a mist, spreading like a gigantic spider's web, was beginning to raise the level of the Buckinghamshire fields. As they walked homewards, it climbed with them, keeping pace with them like a dog; sometimes hurrying ahead, then dropping back, but always with them.

It was exactly five o'clock as they reached Laymer's. Tea was ready. 'Do you still want to go, Jim?' asked Lander abruptly.

'Sure, Bo!' replied Brinton lightly.

'Here's the key,' said Lander, smiling, 'the Open Sesame to the Chamber of Horrors. The electric light is turned off, so all the light we shall have will be produced by my torch. One last word of advice—if you want to get the best chance of a thrill, try to keep your mind quite empty—don't talk as I personally conduct this tour. Concentrate on *not* concentrating.'

'I understand what you mean,' said Brinton.

'Well, then, let's get a move on,' said Lander. An idea suddenly occurred to Brinton. 'How will you be able to show me over it if you've never been inside it ?'

'You needn't worry about that,' replied Lander.

The fog was thick by now, and they wavered slightly as they groped their way down the lane, compressed by high hedges, which led to Pailton. When they reached it, Brinton's eyes turned up to observe the windows on the second floor. And then Lander stepped forward and placed the key in the lock.

As the door swung open, the fog, which seemed to have been crouching at his heels, leapt forward and entered with him and inundated the passage down which he moved. The moment he was inside, something advanced to meet him. He opened a door on the left of the passage and flashed his torch round it. The fog was in there too. Jim, he could feel, was at this elbow.

'This is where they found the burglar—it's the dining room.'

His voice was not quite under control. 'Quite a pleasant room, smells a bit frowsty.' The little beam wandered from chair to desk, settling for a moment here and there. Then he shut the door and stepped along the passage until the little beam revealed a flight of stairs which he began to climb. He still heard Brinton's steps coming up behind him. Up on the first floor he opened another door. 'This is the drawing rooms,' he said. 'the Proctors' cook was found dead here in 1921. Round swung the tiny beam, fastening on chairs, tables, desks, curtains. He shut the door and began to climb another flight of stairs. He could hear Jim's feet pattering up behind him. On the second floor he opened still another door. 'This, my dear Jim, is the nasty one; it was from here Amy Pendexter fell and broke her neck.'

His voice had risen slightly, and he was speaking quickly. Once again he flashed his torch over chairs, tables, curtains, and ahead.

'Well, Jim, do you get any reaction? Do you? You can speak now.' As there was no answer, he turned, and swung the beam of his torch on to the person just behind him. But it wasn't Brinton who was standing at his elbow...

'What's the matter, Willie?' asked Brinton, 'can't you find the keyhole?' The figure in front of him remained motionless 'Can't you find the keyhole?' asked Brinson more urgently. As the figure still remained motionless, Jim Brinton lit a match and peered forward... And then he reeled back.

'Who, in God's name, are you?' he cried.

The White Wolf of the Hartz Mountains

Frederick Marryat

Before noon Philip and Krantz had embarked, and made sail in the peroqua.

They had no difficulty in steering their course; the islands by day, and the clear stars by night, were their compass. It is true that they did not follow the more direct track, but they followed the more secure, working up the smooth waters, and gaining to the northward more than to the west. Many times they were chased by the Malay proas, which infested the islands, but the swiftness of their little peroqua was their security; indeed, the chase was, generally speaking, abandoned as soon as the smallness of the vessel was made out by the pirates, who expected that little or no booty was to be gained.

One morning, as they were sailing between the isles, with less wind than usual, Philip observed—

'Krantz, you said that there were events in your own life, or connected with it, which would corroborate the mysterious tale I confided to you. Will you now tell me to what you referred?'

'Certainly,' replied Krantz; 'I have often thought of doing so, but one circumstance or another has hitherto prevented me; this is, however, a fitting opportunity. Prepare therefore to listen to a strange story, quite as strange, perhaps, as your own.

'I take it for granted that you have heard people speak of the Hartz Mountains,' observed Krantz.

'I have never heard people speak of them, that I can recollect,' replied Philip; 'but I have read of them in some book, and of the strange things which have occurred there.'

'It is indeed a wild region,' rejoined Krantz, 'and many strange tales are told of it; but strange as they are, I have good reason for believing them to be true.

'My father was not born, or originally a resident, in the Hartz Mountains; he was a serf of a Hungarian nobleman, of great possessions, in Transylvania; but although a serf, he was not by any means a poor or illiterate man. In fact, he was rich and his intelligence and respectability were such that he had been raised by his lord to the stewardship; but whoever may happen to be born a serf, a serf must he remain, even though he become a wealthy man: such was the condition of my father. My father had been married for about five years; and by his marriage had three children—my eldest brother Caesar, myself (Hermann), and a sister named Marcella. You know, Philip, that Latin is still the language spoken in that country; and that will account for our high-sounding names. My mother was a very beautiful woman, unfortunately more beautiful than virtuous: she was seen and admired by the lord of the soil; my father was sent away upon some mission; and during his absence, my mother, flattered by the attentions, and won by the assiduities of this nobleman, yielded to his wishes. It so happened that my father returned very unexpectedly, and discovered the intrigue. The evidence of my mother's shame was positive: he surprised her in the company of her seducer! Carried away by the impetuosity of his feelings, he watched the opportunity of a meeting taking place between them, and murdered both his wife and her seducer. Conscious that, as a serf, not even the provocation which he had received would be allowed as a justification of his conduct, he hastily collected together what money he could lay his hands upon, and, as we were then in the depth of winter, he put his horses to the sleigh, and taking his children with him, he set off in the middle of the night, and was far away before the tragical circumstance had transpired. Aware that he would be pursued, and that he had no chance of escape if he remained in any portion of his native country (in which the authorities could lay hold of him), he continued his flight without intermission until he had buried himself in the intricacies and seclusions of the Hartz Mountains. Of course, all that I have now told you I learned afterwards. My oldest recollections are knit to a rude, yet comfortable, cottage in which I lived with my father, brother, and sister. It was on the confines of one of those vast forests which cover the northern part of Germany; around it were a few acres of ground, which, during the summer months, my father cultivated, and which, though they yielded a doubtful harvest, were sufficient for our support. In the winter we remained much indoors, for, as my father followed the chase, we were left alone, and the wolves during that season incessantly prowled about. My father had purchased the cottage, and land about it, off one of the rude foresters, who gain their livelihood partly by hunting and partly by burning charcoal, for the purpose of smelting the ore from the neighbouring mines; it was distant about two miles from any other habitation. I can call to mind the whole landscape now; the tall pines which rose up on the mountain above us, and the wide expanse of the forest beneath, on the topmost boughs and heads of whose trees we looked down from our cottage, as the mountain below us rapidly descended into the distant valley. In summer time the prospect was beautiful; but during the severe winter a more desolate scene could not well be imagined.

'I said that, in the winter, my father occupied himself with the chase; every day he left us, and often would he lock the door, that we might not leave the cottage. He had no one to assist him, or to take care of us—indeed, it was not easy to find a female servant who would live in such a solitude; but, could he have found one, my father would not have received her, for he had imbibed a horror of the sex, as the difference of his conduct towards us, his two boys, and my poor little sister Marcella, evidently proved. You may suppose we were sadly neglected; indeed, we suffered much, for my father, fearful that we might come to some harm, would not allow us fuel when he left the cottage; and we were obliged, therefore, to creep under the heaps of bears' skins, and there to keep ourselves as warm as we could until he returned in the evening, when a blazing fire was our delight. That my father chose this restless sort of life may appear strange, but the fact was that he could not remain quiet; whether from the remorse for having committed murder, or from the misery consequent on his change of situation, or from both combined, he was never happy unless he was in a state of activity. Children, however, when left so much to themselves, acquire a thoughtfulness not common to their age. So it was with us; and during the short cold days of winter, we would sit silent, longing for the happy hours when the snow would melt and the leaves burst out, and the birds begin their songs, and when we should again be set at liberty.

'Such was our peculiar and savage sort of life until my

brother Caesar was nine, myself seven, and my sister five years old, when the circumstances occurred on which is based the extraordinary narrative which I am about to relate.

'One evening my father returned home rather later than usual; he had been unsuccessful, and as the weather was very severe, and many feet of snow were upon the ground, he was not only very cold, but in a very bad humour. He had brought in wood, and we were all three gladly assisting each other in blowing on the embers to create a blaze, when he caught poor little Marcella by the arm and threw her aside; the child fell, struck her mouth, and bled very much. My brother ran to raise her up. Accustomed to ill-usage, and afraid of my father, she did not dare cry, but looked up in his face very piteously. My father drew his stool nearer to the hearth, muttered something in abuse of women, and busied himself with the fire, which both my brother and I had deserted when our sister was so unkindly treated. A cheerful blaze was soon the result of his exertions; but we did not, as usual, crowd round it. Marcella, still bleeding, retired to a corner, and my brother and I took our seats beside her, while my father hung over the fire gloomily and alone. Such had been our position for about half an hour when the howl of a wolf, close under the window of the cottage, fell on our ears. My father started up, and seized his gun; the howl was repeated; he examined the priming, and then hastily left the cottage, shutting the door after him. We all waited (anxiously listening), for we thought that if he succeeded in shooting the wolf, he would return in a better humour; and, although he was harsh to all of us, and particularly so to our little sister, still we loved our father, and loved to see him cheerful and happy, for what else had we to look up to? And I may here observe that perhaps there never were three children who were fonder of each other; we did not, like other children, fight and dispute together; and if, by chance, any disagreement did arise, between my elder brother and me, little Marcella would run to us, and kissing us both, seal, through her entreaties, the peace between us. Marcella was a lovely, amiable child; I can recall her beautiful features even now. Alas! Poor little Marcella.'

'She is dead, then?' observed Philip.

'Dead! Yes, dead! But how did she die? But I must not anticipate, Philip; let me tell my story.'

'We waited for some time, but the report of the gun did not reach us, and my elder brother then said, 'Our father has followed the wolf, and will not be back for some time. Marcella, let us wash the blood from your mouth, and then we will leave this corner and go to the fire to warm ourselves.'

'We did so, and remained there until near midnight, every minute wondering, as it grew later, why our father did not return. We had no idea that he was in any danger, but we thought that he must have chased the wolf for a very long time. "I will look out and see if father is coming," said my brother Caesar, going to the door. "Take care," said Marcella, "the wolves must be about now, and we cannot kill them, brother." My brother opened the door very cautiously, and but a few inches; he peeped out. "I see nothing," said he, after a time, and once more he joined us at the fire. "We have had no supper," said I, for my father usually cooked the meat as soon as he came home; and during his absence we had nothing but the fragments of the preceding day.

'"And if our father comes home, after his hunt, Caesar," said Marcella, "he will be pleased to have some supper; let us cook it for him and for ourselves." Caesar climbed upon the stool, and reached down some meat—I forget now whether it was venison or bear's meat, but we cut off the usual quantity, and proceeded to dress it, as we used to do under our father's superintendence. We were all busy putting it into the platters before the fire, to await his coming, when we heard the sound of a horn. We listened—there was a noise outside, and a minute afterwards my father entered, ushered in a young female and a large dark man in a hunter's dress.

'Perhaps I had better now relate what was only known to me many years afterwards. When my father had left the cottage, he perceived a large white wolf about thirty yards from him; as soon as the animal saw my father, it retreated slowly, growling and snarling. My father followed; the animal did not run, but always kept at some distance; and my father did not like to fire until he was pretty certain that his ball would take effect; thus they went on for some time, the wolf now leaving my father far behind, and then stopping and snarling defiance at him, and then, again, on his approach, setting off at speed.

'Anxious to shoot the animal (for the white wolf is very rare), my father continued the pursuit for several hours, during which he continually ascended the mountain.

'You must know, Philip, that there are peculiar spots on those mountains which are supposed, and, as my story will prove, truly supposed, to be inhabited by the evil influences: they are well known to the huntsmen, who invariably avoid them. Now, one of these spots, an open space in the pine forest above us, had been pointed out to my father as dangerous on that account. But whether he disbelieved these wild stories, or whether, in his eager pursuit of the chase, he disregarded them, I know not; certain, however, it is, that he was decoyed by the white wolf to his open space, when the animal appeared to slacken her speed. My father approached, came close up to her, raised his gun to his shoulder and was about to fire, when the wolf suddenly disappeared. He thought that the snow on the ground must have dazzled his sight, and he let down his gun to look for the beast—but she was gone; how she could have escaped over the clearance, without his seeing her, was beyond his comprehension. Mortified at the ill-success of his chase, he was about to retrace his steps, when he heard the distant sound of a horn. Astonishment at such a sound—at such an hour—in such a wilderness made him forget for the moment his disappointment, and he remained riveted to the spot. In a minute the horn was blown a second time, and at no great distance; my father stood still, and listened; a third time it was blown. I forget the term used to express it, but it was the signal which, my father well knew, implied that the party was lost in the woods. In a few minutes more my father beheld a man on horseback, with a female seated on the crupper, enter the cleared space, and ride up to him. At first, my father called to mind the strange stories which he had heard of the supernatural beings who were said to frequent these mountains; but the nearer approach of the parties satisfied him that they were mortals like himself. As soon as they came up to him, the man who guided the horse accosted him, "Friend hunter, you are out late, the better fortune for us; we have ridden far, and are in fear of our lives, which are eagerly sought after. These mountains have enabled us to elude our pursuers; but if we find not shelter and refreshment, that will avail us little, as we must perish from hunger and the inclemency of the night. My daughter, who rides behind me, is now more dead than alive—say, can you assist us in our difficulty?"

"'My cottage is some few miles distant," replied my father, "but I have little to offer you besides a shelter from the weather;

to the little I have you are welcome. May I ask whence you come?"

"'Yes, friend, it is no secret now; we have escaped from Transylvania, where my daughter's honour and my life were equally in jeopardy!'"

'This information was quite enough to raise an interest in my father's heart. He remembered his own escape: he remembered the loss of his wife's honour, and the tragedy by which it was wound up. He immediately, and warmly, offered all the assistance which he could afford them.

"'There is no time to be lost, then, good sir," observed the horseman; "my daughter is chilled with the frost, and cannot hold out much longer against the severity of the weather."

"'Follow me," replied my father, leading the way towards his home.

"'I was lured away in pursuit of a large white wolf," observed my father; "it came to the very window of my hut, or I should not have been out at this time of night."

"'The creature passed by us just as we came out of the wood," said the female, in a silvery tone.

"'I was nearly discharging my piece at it," observed the hunter; "but since it did us such good service, I am glad that I allowed it to escape."

'In about an hour and a half, during which my father walked at a rapid pace, the party arrived at the cottage, and, as I said before, came in.

"'We are in good time, apparently," observed the dark hunter, catching the smell of the roasted meat, as he walked to the fire and surveyed my brother and sister and myself. "You have young cooks here, Meinheer." "I am glad that we shall not have to wait," replied my father. "Come, seat yourself by the fire; you require warmth after your cold ride." "And where can I put up my horse, Meinheer?" observed the huntsman. "I will take care of him," replied my father, going out of the cottage door.

'The female must, however, be particularly described. She was young, and apparently twenty years of age. She was dressed in a travelling dress, deeply bordered with white fur, and wore a cap of white ermine on her head. Her features were very beautiful, at least I thought so, and so my father has since declared. Her hair was flaxen, glossy, and shining, and bright as a mirror; and her mouth, although somewhat large when it was open, showed the most brilliant teeth I have ever beheld. But there was something about her eyes, bright as they were, which made us children afraid; they were so restless, so furtive; I could not at that time tell why, but I felt as if there was cruelty in her eye; and when she beckoned us to come to her, we approached her with fear and trembling. Still she was beautiful, very beautiful. She spoke kindly to my brother and myself, patted our heads and caressed us; but Marcella would not come near her; on the contrary, she slunk away, and hid herself in bed, and would not wait for the supper, which half an hour before she had been so anxious for.

'My father, having put the horse into a close shed, soon returned, and supper was placed on the table. When it was over, my father requested the young lady take possession of the bed, and he would remain at the fire, and sit up with her father. After some hesitation on her part, this arrangement was agreed to, and I and my brother crept into the other bed with Marcella, for we had as yet always slept together.

'But we could not sleep; there was something so unusual, not only in seeing strange people, but in having those people

sleep at the cottage, that we were bewildered. As for poor little
Marcella, she was quiet, but I perceived that she trembled during
the whole night, and sometimes I thought that she was checking
a sob. My father had brought out some spirits, which he rarely
used, and he and the strange hunter remained drinking and
talking before the fire. Our ears were ready to catch the slightest
whisper—so much was our curiosity excited.

"'You said you came from Transylvania?" observed my
father.

"'Even so, Meinheer," replied the hunter. "I was a serf to
the noble house; my master would insist upon my surrendering
up my fair girl to his wishes; it ended in my giving him a few
inches of my hunting-knife."

"'We are countrymen and brothers in misfortune," replied
my father, taking the huntsman's hand and pressing it warmly.

"'Indeed! Are you then from that country?"

"'Yes; and I too have fled for my life. But mine is a melancholy
tale."

"'Your name?" inquired the hunter.

"'Krantz."

"'What! I have heard your tale; you need not renew your
grief by repeating it now. Welcome, most welcome, Meinheer,
and, I may say, my worthy kinsman. I am your second cousin,
Wilfred of Barnsdorf," cried the hunter, raising up and
embracing my father.

'They filled their horn-mugs to the brim, and drank to one
another after the German fashion. The conversation was then
carried on in a low tone; all that we could collect from it was
that our new relative and his daughter were to take up their
abode in our cottage, at least for the present. In about an hour
they both fell back in their chairs and appeared to sleep.

'"Marcella, dear, did you hear?" said my brother, in a low tone.

'"Yes," replied Marcella, in a whisper, "I heard all. Oh! brother, I cannot bear to look upon that woman—I feel so frightened."

'My brother made no reply, and shortly afterwards we were all three fast asleep.

'When we awoke the next morning, we found that the hunter's daughter had risen before us. I thought she looked more beautiful than ever. She came up to little Marcella and caressed her; the child burst into tears, and sobbed as if her heart would break.

'But not to detain you with too long a story, the huntsman and his daughter were accommodated in the cottage. My father and he went out hunting daily, leaving Christina with us. She performed all the household duties; was very kind to us children; and gradually the dislike even of little Marcella wore away. But a great change took place in my father; he appeared to have conquered his aversion to the sex, and was most attentive to Christina. Often, after her father and we were in bed, would he sit up with her, conversing in a low tone by the fire. I ought to have mentioned that my father and the huntsman Wilfred slept in another portion of the cottage, and that the bed which he formerly occupied, and which was in the same room as ours, had been given up to the use of Christina. These visitors had been about three weeks at the cottage, when, one night, after we children had been sent to bed, a consultation was held. My father had asked Christina in marriage, and had obtained both her own consent and that of Wilfred; after this, a conversation took place, which was, as nearly as I can recollect, as follows—

'"You may take my child, Meinheer Krantz, and my blessing

with her, and I shall then leave you and seek some other habitation—it matters little where."

"'Why not remain here, Wilfred?"

"'No, no, I am called elsewhere; let that suffice, and ask no more questions. You have my child."

"'I thank you for her, and will duly value her but there is one difficulty."

"'I know what you would say; there is no priest here in this wild country; true; neither is there any law to bind. Still must some ceremony pass between you, to satisfy a father. Will you consent to marry her after my fashion? If so, I will marry you directly."

"'I will," replied my father.

"'Then take her by the hand. Now, Meinheer, swear."

"'I swear," repeated my father.

"'By all the spirits of the Hartz Mountains—"

"'Nay, why not by Heaven?" interrupted my father.

"'Because it is not my humour," rejoined Wilfred. "If I prefer that oath, less binding, perhaps, than another, surely you will not thwart me."

"'Well, be it so, then; have your humour. Will you make me swear by that in which I do not believe?"

"'Yet many do so, who in outward appearance are Christians," rejoined Wilfred; "say, will you be married, or shall I take my daughter away with me?'

"'Proceed," replied my father impatiently.

"'I swear by all the spirits of the Hartz Mountains, by all their power for good or for evil, that I take Christina for my wedded wife; that I will ever protect her, cherish her, and love her; that my hand shall never be raised against her to harm her."

'My father repeated the words after Wilfred.

"'And if I fail in this my vow, may all the vengeance of the spirits fall upon me and upon my children; may they perish by the vulture, by the wolf, or other beasts of the forest; may their flesh be torn from their limbs, and their bones blanch in the wilderness: all this I swear."

My father hesitated, as he repeated the last words; little Marcella could not restrain herself, and as my father repeated the last sentence, she burst into tears. This sudden interruption appeared to discompose the party, particularly my father; he spoke harshly to the child, who controlled her sobs, burying her face under the bedclothes.

'Such was the second marriage of my father. The next morning, the hunter Wilfred mounted his horse and rode away.

'My father resumed his bed, which was in the same room as ours; and things went on much as before the marriage, except that our new stepmother did not show any kindness towards us; indeed, during my father's absence, she would often beat us, particularly little Marcella, and her eyes would flash fire, as she looked eagerly upon the fair and lovely child.

'One night my sister awoke me and my brother.

"'What is the matter?" said Caesar.

"'She has gone out," whispered Marcella.

"'Gone out!"

"'Yes, gone out at the door, in her nightclothes," replied the child; "I saw her get out of bed, look at my father to see if he slept, and then she went out the door."

'What could induce her to leave her bed, and all undressed to go out, in such bitter wintry weather, with the snow deep on the ground, was to us incomprehensible; we lay awake, and in about an hour we heard the growl of a wolf close under the window.

"'There is a wolf," said Caesar. "She will be torn to pieces."

'"Oh, no!" cried Marcella.

'In a few minutes our stepmother appeared; she was in her nightdress, as Marcella had stated. She let down the latch of the door, so as to make no noise, went to a pail of water, and washed her face and hands, and then slipped into the bed where my father lay.

'We all three trembled—we hardly knew why; but we resolved to watch the next night. We did so; and not only on the ensuing night, but on many others, and always at about the same hour would our stepmother rise from her bed and leave the cottage; and after she was gone we invariably heard the growl of a wolf under our window, and always saw her on her return wash herself before she retired to bed. We observed also that she seldom sat down to meals, and that when she did she appeared to eat with dislike; but when the meat was taken down to be prepared for dinner, she would often furtively put a raw piece into her mouth.

'My brother Caesar was a courageous boy; he did not like to speak to my father until he knew more. He resolved that he would follow her out, and ascertain what she did. Marcella and I endeavoured to dissuade him from the project; but he would not be controlled; and the very next night he lay down in his clothes, and as soon as our stepmother had left the cottage he jumped up, took down my father's gun, and followed her.

'You may imagine in what a state of suspense Marcella and I remained during his absence. After a few minutes we heard the report of a gun. It did not awaken my father; and we lay trembling with anxiety. In a minute afterwards we saw our stepmother enter the cottage—her dress was bloody. I put my hand to Marcella's mouth to prevent her crying out, although I was myself in great alarm. Our stepmother approached my father's bed, looked to see if he was asleep, and then went to the chimney and blew up the embers into a blaze.

'"Who is there?" said my father, waking up.

'"Lie still, dearest," replied my stepmother; "it is only me; I have lighted the fire to warm some water; I am not quite well."

'My father turned round, and was soon asleep; but we watched our stepmother. She changed her linen, and threw the garments she had worn into the fire; and we then perceived that her right leg was bleeding profusely, as if from a gunshot wound. She bandaged it up, and then dressing herself remained before the fire until the break of day.

'Poor little Marcella, her heart beat quick as she pressed me to her side—so indeed did mine. Where was our brother Caesar? How did my stepmother receive the wound unless from his gun? At last my father rose, and then for the first time I spoke, saying, "Father, where is my brother Caesar?"

'"Your brother?" exclaimed he; "why, where can he be?"

'"Merciful Heaven! I thought as I lay very restless last night," observed our stepmother, "that I heard somebody open the latch of the door; and, dear me, husband, what has become of your gun?"

'My father cast his eyes up above the chimney, and perceived that his gun was missing for a moment he looked perplexed; then, seizing a broad axe, he went out of the cottage without saying another world.

'He did not remain away from us long; in a few minutes he returned, bearing in his arms the mangled body of my poor brother; he laid it down, and covered up his face.

'My stepmother rose up, and looked at the body, while Marcella and I threw ourselves by its side, wailing and sobbing bitterly.

'"Go to bed again, children," said she sharply. "Husband," continued she, "your boy must have taken the gun down to shoot a wolf, and the animal has been too powerful for him. Poor boy! He has paid dearly for his rashness."

'My father made no reply. I wished to speak—to tell all—but Marcella, who perceived my intention, held me by the arm, and looked at me so imploringly, that I desisted.

'My father, therefore, was left in his error; but Marcella and I, although we could not comprehend it, were conscious that our stepmother was in some way connected with my brother's death.

'That day my father went out and dug a grave; and when he laid the body in the earth he piled up stones over it, so that the wolved should not be able to dig it up. The shock of this catastrophe was to my poor father very severe; for several days he never went to the chase, although at times he would utter bitter anathemas and vengeance against the wolves.

'But during this time of mourning on his part, my stepmother's nocturnal wanderings continued with the same regularity as before.

'At last my father took down his gun to repair to the forest; but he soon returned, and appeared much annoyed.

'"Would you believe it, Christina, that the wolves—perdition to the whole race!—have actually contrived to dig up the body of my poor boy, and now there is nothing left of him but his bones."

'"Indeed!" replied my stepmother. Marcella looked at me, and I saw in her intelligent eye all she would have uttered.

'"A wolf growls under our window every night, father," said I.

'"Ay, indeed! Why did you not tell me, boy? Wake me the

next time you hear it."

'I saw my stepmother turn away; her eyes flashed fire, and she gnashed her teeth.

'My father went out again, and covered up with a larger pile of stones the little remains of my poor brother which the wolves had spared. Such was the first act of the tragedy.

'The spring now came on; the snow disappeared, and we were permitted to leave the cottage; but never would I quit for one moment my dear little sister, to whom, since the death of my brother, I was more ardently attached than ever; indeed, I was afraid to leave her alone with my stepmother, who appeared to have a particular pleasure in ill-treating the child. My father was now employed upon his little farm, and I was able to render him some assistance.

'Marcella used to sit by us while we were at work, leaving my stepmother alone in the cottage. I ought to observe that, as the spring advanced, so did my stepmother decrease her nocturnal rambles, and that we never heard the growl of the wolf under the window after I had spoken of it to my father.

'One day, when my father and I were in the field, Marcella being with us, my stepmother came out, saying that she was going into the forest to collect some herbs that my father wanted, and that Marcella must go to the cottage and watch the dinner. Marcella went; and my stepmother soon disappeared in the forest, taking a direction quite contrary to that in which the cottage stood, and leaving my father and me, as it were, between her and Marcella.

'About an hour afterwards we were startled by shrieks from the cottage—evidently the shrieks of little Marcella. "Marcella has burnt herself, father," said I, throwing down my spade. My father threw down his, and we both hastened to the cottage. Before we could gain the door, out darted a large white wolf, which fled with the utmost celerity. My father had no weapon; he rushed into the cottage, and there saw poor little Marcella expiring. Her body was dreadfully mangled and the blood pouring from it had formed a large pool on the cottage floor. My father's first intention had been to seize his gun and pursue; but he was checked by this horrid spectacle; he knelt down by his dying child, and burst into tears. Marcella could just look kindly on us for a few seconds, and then her eyes were closed in death.

'My father and I were still hanging over my poor sister's body when my stepmother came in. At the dreadful sight she expressed much concern; but she did not appear to recoil from the sight of blood, as most people do.

'"Poor child!" said she, "it must have been that great white wolf which passed me just now, and frightened me so. She's quite dead, Krantz."

'"I know it!—I know it!" cried my father, in agony.

'I thought my father would never recover from the effects of this second tragedy; he mourned bitterly over the body of his sweet child, and for several days would not consign it to its grave, although frequently requested by my stepmother to do so. At last he yielded, and dug a grave for her close by that of my poor brother, and took every precaution that the wolves should not violate her remains.

'I was now really miserable as I lay alone in the bed which I had formerly shared with my brother and sister. I could not help thinking that my stepmother was implicated in both their deaths, although I could not account for the manner; but I no longer felt afraid of her; my little heart was full of hatred and revenge.

'The night after my sister had been buried, as I lay awake,

I perceived my stepmother get up and go out of the cottage. I waited some time, then dressed myself, and looked out through the door, which I half opened. The moon shone bright, and I could see the spot where my brother and my sister had been buried; and what was my horror when I perceived my stepmother busily removing the stones from Marcella's grave!

'She was in her white nightdress, and the moon shone full upon her. She was digging with her hands, and throwing away the stones behind her with all the ferocity of a wild beast. It was some time before I could collect my senses and decide what I should do. At last I perceived that she had arrived at the body, and raised it up to the side of the grave. I could bear it no longer: I ran to my father and awoke him.

'"Father, father!" cried I, "dress yourself, and get your gun."

'"What!" cried my father, "the wolves are there, are they?"

'He jumped out of bed, threw on his clothes, and in his anxiety did not appear to perceive the absence of his wife. As soon as he was ready, I opened the door; he went out, and I followed him.

'Imagine his horror, when (unprepared as he was for such a sight) he beheld, as he advanced towards the grave, not a wolf, but his wife, in her nightdress, on her hands and knees, crouching by the body of my sister, and tearing off large pieces of flesh, and devouring them with all the avidity of a wolf. She was too busy to be aware of our approach. My father dropped his gun; his hair stood on end, so did mine; he breathed heavily, and then his breath for a time stopped. I picked up the gun and put it into his hand. Suddenly he appeared as if concentrated rage had restored him to double vigour; he levelled his piece, fired, and with a loud shriek down fell the wretch whom he had fostered in his bosom.

'"God of heaven!" cried my father, sinking down upon the earth in a swoon, as soon as he had discharged his gun.

'I remained some time by his side before he recovered. "Where am I?" said he, "What has happened? Oh!—yes, yes! I recollect now. Heaven forgive me!"

'He rose and we walked up to the grave; imagine our astonishment and horror to find that, instead of the dead body of my stepmother, as we expected, there was, lying over the remains of my poor sister, a large white she-wolf.

'"The white wolf," exclaimed my father, "the white wolf which decoyed me into the forest—I see it all now—I have dealt with the spirits of the Hartz Mountains."

'For some time my father remained in silence and deep thought. He then carefully lifted the body of my sister, replaced it in the grave, and covered it over as before, having struck the head of the dead animal with the heel of his boot, and raving like a madman. He walked back to the cottage, shut the door, and threw himself on the bed; I did the same, for I was in a stupor of amazement.

'Early in the morning we were both roused by a loud knocking at the door, and in rushed the hunter Wilfred.

'"My daughter—man—my daughter!—where is my daughter?" cried he in a rage.

'"Where the wretch, the fiend should be, I trust," replied my father, starting up, and displaying equal choler: "where she should be—in hell! Leave this cottage, or you may fare worse."

'"Ha—ha!" replied the hunter, "would you harm a potent spirit of the Hartz Mountains? Poor mortal, who must needs wed a werewolf."

'"Out, demon! I defy thee and thy power."

'"Yet shall you feel it; remember your oath—your solemn

oath—never to raise your hand against her to harm her."

"'I made no compact with evil spirits."

"'You did, and if you failed in your vow, you were to meet the vengeance of the spirits. Your children were to perish by the vulture, the wolf—"

"'Out, out, demon!'"

"'And their bones blanch in the wilderness. Ha—ha!'"

'My father, frantic with rage, seized his axe and raised it over Wilfred's head to strike.

"'All this I swear," continued the huntsman mockingly.

'The axe descended; but it passed through the form of the hunter, and my father lost his balance, and fell heavily on the floor.

"'Mortal!" said the hunter, striding over my father's body, "We have power over those only who have committed murder. You have been guilty of a double murder: you shall pay the penalty attached to your marriage vow. Two of your children are gone, the third is yet to follow—and follow them he will, for your oath is registered. Go—it were kindness to kill thee—your punishment is, that you live!"

'With these words the spirit disappeared. My father rose from the floor, embraced me tenderly, and knelt down in prayer.

'The next morning he quitted the cottage for ever. He took me with him, and bent his steps to Holland, where we safely arrived. He had some little money with him; but he had not been many days in Amsterdam before he was seized with a brain fever, and died raving mad. I was put into the asylum, and afterwards was sent to sea before the mast. You now know all my history. The question is, whether I am to pay the penalty of my father's oath? I am myself perfectly convinced that, in some way or another, I shall.'

II

On the twenty-second day the high land of the south of Sumatra was in view: as there were no vessels in sight, they resolved to keep their course through the Straits, and run for Pulo Penang, which they expected, as their vessel lay so close to the wind, to reach in seven or eight days. By constant exposure Philip and Krantz were now so bronzed that with their long beards and Mussulman dresses, they might easily have passed off for natives. They had steered during the whole of the days exposed to a burning sun; they had lain down and slept in the dew of the night; but their health had not suffered. But for several days, since he had confided the history of his family to Philip, Krantz had become silent and melancholy; his usual flow of spirits had vanished, and Philip had often questioned him as to the cause. As they entered the Straits, Philip talked of what they should do upon their arrival at Goa; when Krantz gravely replied, 'For some days, Philip, I have had a presentiment that I shall never see that city.'

'You are out of health, Krantz,' replied Philip.

'No, I am in sound health, body and mind. I have endeavoured to shake off the presentiment, but in vain; there is a warning voice that continually tells me that I shall not be long with you Philip; will you oblige me by making me content on one point? I have gold about my person which may be useful to you; oblige me by taking it, and securing it on your own.'

'What nonsense, Krantz.'

'It is no nonsense, Philip. Have you not had your warnings? Why should I not have mine? You know that I have little fear in my composition, and that I care not about death; but I feel the presentiment which I speak of more strongly every hour...'

'These are the imaginings of a disturbed brain, Krantz; why you, young, in full health and vigour, should not pass your days in peace, and live to a good old age, there is no cause for believing. You will be better tomorrow.'

'Perhaps so,' replied Krantz; 'but you still must yield to my whim, and take the gold. If I am wrong, and we do arrive safe, you know, Philip, you can let me have it back,' observed Krantz, with a faint smile—'but you forget, our water is nearly out, and we must look out for a rill on the coast to obtain a fresh supply.'

'I was thinking of that when you commenced this unwelcome topic. We had better look out for the water before dark, and as soon as we have replenished our jars, we will make sail again.'

At the time that this conversation took place, they were on the eastern side of the Strait, about forty miles to the northward. The interior of the coast was rocky and mountainous, but it slowly descended to low lands of alternate forest and jungles, which continued to the beach; the country appeared to be uninhabited. Keeping close in to the shore, they discovered, after two hours' run, a fresh stream which burst in a cascade from the mountains, and swept its devious course through the jungle, until it poured its tribute into the waters of the Strait.

They ran close into the mouth of the stream, lowered the sails, and pulled the peroqua against the current until they had advanced far enough to assure them that the water was quite fresh. The jars were soon filled, and they were again thinking of pushing off, when enticed by the beauty of the spot, the coolness of the fresh water, and wearied with their long confinement on board of the peroqua, they proposed to bathe—a luxury hardly to be appreciated by those who have not been in a similar situation. They threw off their Mussulman dresses, and plunged into the stream, where they remained for some time. Krantz was the first to get out; he complained of feeling chilled, and he walked on to the banks where their clothes had been laid. Philip also approached nearer to the beach, intending to follow him.

'And now, Philip,' said Krantz, 'this will be a good opportunity for me to give you the money. I will open my sash and pour it out, and you can put it into your own before you put it on.'

Philip was standing in the water, which was about level with his waist.

'Well, Krantz,' said he, 'I suppose if it must be so, it must; but it appears to me an idea so ridiculous—however, you shall have your own way.'

Philip quitted the run, and sat down by Krantz, who was already busy in shaking the doubloons out of the folds of his sash; at last he said—

'I believe, Philip, you have got them all, now? I feel satisfied.'

'What danger there can be to you, which I am not equally exposed to, I cannot conceive,' replied Philip: 'however—'

Hardly had he said these words, when there was a tremendous roar—a rush like a mighty wind through the air—a blow which threw him on his back—a loud cry—and a contention. Philip recovered himself, and perceived the naked form of Krantz carried off with the speed of an arrow by an enormous tiger through the jungle. He watched with distended eyeballs; in a few seconds the animal and Krantz had disappeared.

'God of Heaven! Would that Thou hadst spared me this,' cried Philip, throwing himself down in agony on his face. 'O Krantz! My friend—my brother—too sure was your presentiment. Merciful God! Have pity—but Thy will be done.' And Philip burst into a flood of tears.

For more than an hour did he remain fixed upon the

spot, careless and indifferent to the danger by which he was surrounded. At last, somewhat recovered, he rose, dressed himself, and then again sat down—his eyes fixed upon the clothes of Krantz, and the gold which still lay on the sand.

'He would give me that gold. He foretold his doom. Yes! Yes! It was his destiny, and it has been fulfilled. His bones will bleach in the wilderness, and the spirit-hunter and his wolfish daughter are avenged.'

Gone Fishing

Ruskin Bond

The house was called 'Undercliff', because that's where it stood—under a cliff. The man who went away—the owner of the house was Robert Astley. And the man who stayed behind—the old family retainer—was Prem Bahadur.

Astley had been gone many years. He was still a bachelor in his late thirties when he'd suddenly decided that he wanted adventure, romance, faraway places; and he'd given the keys of the house to Prem Bahadur—who'd served the family for thirty years—and had set off on his travels.

Someone saw him in Sri Lanka. He'd been heard of in Burma, around the ruby mines at Mogok. Then he turned up in Java, seeking a passage through the Sunda Straits. After that the trail petered out. Years passed. The house in the hill station remained empty.

But Prem Bahadur was still there, living in an outhouse.

Every day he opened up Undercliff, dusted the furniture in all the rooms, made sure that the bedsheets and pillowcases were clean, and set out Astley's dressing gown and slippers. In the old days, whenever Astley had come home after a journey or a long tramp in the hills, he had liked to bathe and change into his gown and slippers, no matter what the hour. Prem Bahadur still kept them ready. He was convinced that Robert would return one day.

Astley himself had said so.

'Keep everything ready for me, Prem, old chap. I may be back after a year, or two years, or even longer, but I'll be back, I promise you. On the first of every month I want you to go to my lawyer, Mr Kapoor. He'll give you your salary and any money that's needed for the rates and repairs. I want you to keep the house tip-top?'

'Will you bring back a wife, Sahib?'

'Lord, no! Whatever put that idea in your head?'

'I thought, perhaps—because you wanted the house kept ready...'

'Ready for me, Prem. I don't want to come home and find the old place falling down.'

And so Prem had taken care of the house—although there was no news from Astley. What had happened to him? The mystery provided a talking point whenever local people met on the Mall. And in the bazaar the shopkeepers missed Astley because he was a man who spent freely.

His relatives still believed him to be alive. Only a few months back a brother had turned up—a brother who had a farm—in Canada and could not stay in India for long. He had deposited a further sum with the lawyer and told Prem to carry on as before. The salary provided Prem with his few needs. Moreover, he was convinced that Robert would return.

Another man might have neglected the house and grounds, but not Prem Bahadur. He had a genuine regard for the absent owner. Prem was much older—now almost sixty and none too strong, suffering from pleurisy and other chest troubles—but he remembered Robert as both a boy and a young man. They had been together on numerous hunting and fishing trips in the mountains. They had slept out under the stars, bathed in icy mountain streams, and eaten from the same cooking pot. Once, when crossing a small river, they had been swept downstream by a flash flood, a wall of water that came thundering down the gorges without any warning during the rainy season. Together they had struggled back to safety. Back in the hill station, Astley told everyone that Prem had saved his life; while Prem was equally insistent that he owed his life to Robert.

This year the monsoon had begun early and ended late. It dragged on through most of September, and Prem Bahadur's cough grew worse and his breathing more difficult.

He lay on his charpai on the veranda, staring out at the garden, which was beginning to get out of hand, a tangle of dahlias, snake-lilies and convolvulus. The sun finally came out. The wind shifted from the south-west to the north-west, and swept the clouds away.

Prem Bahadur had taken his charpai into the garden, and was lying in the sun, puffing at his small hookah, when he saw Robert Astley at the gate.

He tried to get up but his legs would not oblige him. The hookah slipped from his hand.

Astley came walking down the garden path and stopped in front of the old retainer, smiling down at him. He did not look a day older than when Prem Bahadur had last seen him.

'So you have come at last,' said Prem.

'I told you I'd return.'

'It has been many years. But you have not changed.'

'Nor have you, old chap.'

'I have grown old and sick and feeble.'

'You'll be fine now. That's why I've come.'

'I'll open the house,' said Prem, and this time he found himself getting up quite easily.

'It isn't necessary' said Astley.

'But all is ready for you.'

'I know. I have heard of how well you have looked after everything. Come then, let's take a last look round. We cannot stay, you know.'

Prem was a little mystified but he opened the front door and took Robert through the drawing rooms and up the stairs to the bedroom. Robert saw the dressing gown and the slippers, and he placed his hand gently on the old man's shoulder.

When they returned downstairs and emerged into the sunlight, Prem was surprised to see himself—or rather his skinny body—stretched out on the charpai. The hookah lay on the ground, where it had fallen.

Prem looked at Astley in bewilderment.

'But who is that—lying there?'

'It was you. Only the husk now, the empty shell. This is the real you, standing here beside me.'

'You came for me?'

'I couldn't come until you were ready. As for me, I left my shell a long time ago. But you were determined to hang on, keeping this house together. Are you ready now?'

'And the house?'

'Others will live in it. Nothing is lost for ever, everything begins again. But come, it's time to go fishing...'

Astley took Prem by the arm, and they walked through the dappled sunlight under the deodars and finally left that place for another.